Mudrooroo was born in Narrogin in Western Australia in 1938. He has travelled extensively throughout Australia and the world and is now living in Bungawalbyn in northern New South Wales with his actress-artist wife, Humi. Mudrooroo is active in Aboriginal cultural affairs, is a Member of the Aboriginal Arts Unit committee of the Australia Council, and was a co-founder with Jack Davis of the Aboriginal Writers, Oral Literature and Dramatists Association. He piloted Aboriginal literature courses at Murdoch University, the University of Queensland, the University of the Northern Territory and Bond University. Mudrooroo is a prolific writer of poetry and prose and is best known for his novel, *Wildcat Falling*, and his critical work, *Writing from the Fringe*. At present he is working on a new novel which will be set in India where he lived for seven years, three of which he spent as a Buddhist monk.

Master of the GHOST DREAMING

a novel by
MUDROOROO

An imprint of HarperCollins*Publishers*

AN ANGUS & ROBERTSON BOOK

First published in Australia in 1991 by
Collins/Angus & Robertson Publishers Australia

Collins/Angus & Robertson Publishers Australia
A division of HarperCollinsPublishers (Australia) Pty Limited
Unit 4, Eden Park, 31 Waterloo Road, North Ryde
NSW 2113, Australia

William Collins Publishers Ltd
31 View Road, Glenfield, Auckland 10, New Zealand

Angus & Robertson (UK)
16 Golden Square, London W1R 4BN, United Kingdom

National Library of Australia
Cataloguing-in-Publication data:

Nyoongah, Mudrooroo, 1938–
  Master of the ghost dreaming.
  ISBN 0 207 16952 7.
  I. Title.

A823.3

Typeset in 11/12pt Baskerville by Midland Typesetters, Victoria
Printed in Australia by Globe Press
Cover: Purrukuparli and Pima by Declan Apuatimi,
held in the Patakijiyali Heritage Museum, Bathurst Island,
NT. Photograph by Heide Smith.

5 4 3 2 1
95 94 93 92 91 90

Dedicated to my sweetest 'enemy', Humi

ACKNOWLEDGEMENTS

The verses quoted throughout this novel are from 'The Convict Maid' (published as a broadsheet in London in 1837), and the ballad, 'Van Diemen's Land'.

I

Once, Morning Star had shifted from its course and had drifted far from the dawn. It continued to shine, continued to be a beacon, but became not the harbinger of the morning, of the light, but a marker of the density of the night which has overtaken us. It illuminates our misery and tugs our souls far from day. Our spirits roam the realm of the ghosts—an unfriendly land where trees and plants, insects and serpents, animals and humans wither and suffer.

Now, we, the pitiful fragments of once strong families suffer on in exile. Pulled by Evening Star into the realm of ghosts, only some of us live on, kept alive by our hope that we shall escape this plane of fear and pain. All around us is the darkness of the night; all around us is an underlying silence of a land of death. Where are the crescendos of Cicada; the watching eyes of Kangaroo; the scuffling of Bandicoot? They have been swept from this land. All are gone. Only Crow, he the one close to death and corpses, remains to gloat over us—we, the ones surrounded by death. Surrounded by ghosts, worse, in the arms of ghosts we die to ourselves. And even in that death, there is no surcease. Lost is the way to the skyland. Our souls wander forlornly in the land of ghosts. Our spirits become their play things; our bodies their food, to be ripped apart, and our gnawed bones are scattered. We are in despair; we are sickening unto death; we call to be healed. Anxiously we wait for the ceremony to begin. We wait for our mapan, the Master of the Ghost Dreaming to deliver us. From him we demand release from the land of ghosts. We demand *healing from our shaman, Jangamuttuk: he who is the custodian of the Ghost Dreaming; he who can sing the way of release through song . . .*

Thus Jangamuttuk interpreted the collective feelings of his people, as he waited for the correct moment to begin the ceremony. The feeling needed to rise just as the Hunter had to move the line of his spear towards Wombat. Now . . .

The rap-rap, rap-rap of his clapsticks shattered the silence of the darkness. The sharp raps disappeared out and out, hit some obstruction and circled returning. Rap-rap, rap-rap. Instantly fires were kindled. Little flames flickered, grew stronger with the chant completing the square. 'Fire, flickering, flame grows, flame grows.' Now the square clearing was outlined by the fires. Jangamuttuk's tribespeople stood in a solemn row.

Male and female moved next to each other. The males were naked except for the initiated men who proudly wore the incised pubic shell of their clans; the women subjected to the new Christian faith wore a long skirt, but above their waist to perfect the ceremony, they had painted in a lattice work of white lines that which signified a bodice lowcut as in formal European wear. There was even the appearance of a necklace dangling above the cleavage of the breasts. Three white rows of dots flowed dripping down to just above the three cicatrices of womanhood, passing across the cleavage. In the dip, outlined in red ochre, but appearing dark to invisible in the light of the flames was an eye-shape. To complete their costume, they wore flowers and leafy twigs plaited into their hair and shaped like European women's hats.

The men's head ornamentation also signified the European. Civilisation had shorn many. Gone were the elaborate and proud hairstyles of the initiated men. Now they covered up their naked shame under woollen caps; thus replacing the reality for the symbolic. Those few newcomers who had been spared the clip-clipping of Fada's scissors, arranged their locks into the shape of flat European hats, or piled their hair up around a piece of wood or rolled up cloth so that it might appear in the fire light to be the high helmet of a European soldier. Their body painting had been designed to signify European fashion, both civilian and military. The stripes of military jackets were painted across chests; lapels and buttons, even pockets had been painted with an attention to detail that was quite startling—that is if there were European eyes present to be startled; but for the moment there were none, and even if there had been, it was highly doubtful that the signifiers could have been read. What was the ultimate in a sign system, might still be read as primitive.

Jangamuttuk, dreamer of the ceremony, was painted in like fashion. His work was more elaborate and detailed. A hatch design of red and white encircled his neck in a symbolic collar. Below this were painted the broad lapels of a frockcoat. Four buttons of a spiral design kept the coat closed, and in the vee, the top of a waistcoat peeped out. His legs, and the legs of the male dancers, were painted white with a circular design at the knee.

Now Jangamuttuk, creator and choreographer, checked the company for flaws before the body of the ceremony began. He was not after a realist copy, after all he had no intention of aping the European, but sought for an adaptation of these alien cultural forms appropriate to his own cultural matrix. It was an exciting concept; but it was more than this. There was a ritual need for it to be done. The need for the inclusion of these elements into a ceremony with a far different purpose than mere art. He, the shaman, and purported Master of the Ghost Dreaming, was about to undertake entry into the realm of the ghosts. Not only was he to attempt the act of possession, but he hoped to bring

3

all of his people into contact with the ghost realm so that they could capture the essence of health and well-being, and then break back safely into their own culture and society. This was the purpose of the ceremony. A ceremony which had been dreamt in response to the pleas of his people. He would establish contact. He would enable them to evade the demons of sickness which were weakening and destroying them, and then when they were strong . . . but first the ceremony, but first the ceremony.

The master sang to his clapsticks, asking them to allow him entry into their spirit, begging them to sound the necessary rhythms which were important to his craft. They acknowledged him in the rap-rap, rap-rap of a traditional rhythm. The didgeridoo players followed the sharpness of the rhythm, swooping down on it and rising above, or below as their instruments desired. Each didgeridoo player, Jangamuttuk knew, was letting his instrument speak. Now his clapsticks, anxious for direction stopped; the didgeridoos groaned low and hesitated: this was ceremony, serious business. Jangamuttuk took control of his clapsticks. He entered into a rhythm which switched the playing back onto the individual skills of the musicians. They edged into the time, feeling out the possibilities of the play as the rhythm bounced the shaman towards possession and his people into a new kind of dance.

The dancers clasped each other and began a European reel. They kept to the repetitive steps and let the strange rhythm move their feet. It became their master. Each generation including the tragically few children jigged as Jangamuttuk began to sing in perfect ghost accents:

'They made of me
A ghost down under,
Made for me

4

A place to plunder,
A place to plunder,
Way down under.'

He finished the verse and began again, picking out individual words in the traditional style. This was far from a euphonious rendering, but it was difficult to range vowels and consonants into an harmonious whole in the ghost language he was using. He finished on the words:

'Made me made me mad
Ghost place ghost face
Ghost ghost ghost ghost.'

Feeling his consciousness beginning to slip, feeling the night and the dancers begin to . . . He began the second stanza:

'They made of me
A ghost down under,
Gave me a dram,
It tasted like cram;
Real as my dream,
Way, way under.

Under, plunder, thunder,
Way, may, nay, stay
Down, town, down,
Ghost ghost under,
Slam clam ram mam . . . '

Mada writhed uneasily, then jerked awake as the burning pain hit her. It began way down in her abdomen and twisted along her spasming bowels. She lay there, desperately trying to come to grips with yet another manifestation of what she had come to accept as her pain, her anguish, her hatred and loathing at being forced

5

to continue living on in this awful colony, isolated far from the nearest decent-sized town on a dreary island, where the weather lurched from violent extreme to violent extreme. No wonder her health suffered, no wonder— and that great clod of her husband didn't care one iota, nor did her oaf of a son. He never thought of the sacrifices she had made just in bringing him into the world, and both father and son certainly never considered how isolated she felt in this savage land. But she couldn't blame her son, as that lump beside her was the cause of all their, of all her problems, of her constant state of ill-health. He didn't care for her at all. It was his meddling in things beyond him that had caused her pain.

The constant burning pulsing of her bowels didn't allow her the luxury of contemplating her plight in an uncaring land covered with the secretness of the night. Beyond the drawn, thick curtains the alien stars shone and the pain-laden wind rustled the foreboding trees in the threatening forest. The trees pressed in on the civilised square in which lay the mission house, the chapel, the storerooms and the compound for Christianising the natives, before their corpses went to add to the ever increasing number of graves in the cemetery. Too often all this tugged her into depression, but at the moment none of it bothered her. She was safely hidden away behind thick curtains in a refuge which, as much as possible, resembled the imagined sweetness of her sweet home, with its heavy imported furniture and knick-knacks, far across the ocean. She sighed alone in exile and with the pain eating away at her. She needed her medicine. Over the years her memories of London had dimmed. Now it was a fairyland free from suffering. How she hated that pig of a husband snorting beside her. Him and his career and his excuse of waiting time out only for the pittance of a pension which would be her deliverance. Him and his altruism. His stupid ideas about serving humanity and taking the message of Christian caring and goodwill to benighted savages like the ones dying all around her. Why, he loved those sable friends of his more than he loved his own wife. He didn't care one penny for her and how she suffered. She needed the care of expert doctors that could only be found at home, London! There, she had been in the full bloom of health. Illness had begun when she allowed herself to be taken to this colony—to be lodged in a rough establishment and forced there to raise a son, while the father evaded his responsibilities and roamed across the wilderness on what he called his mission of conciliation.

She had had to be the man to her child while he was off in the wilderness up to God alone knows. Now, after all that time of strength, her body had broken down. It was constantly racked by pain. In fact it felt as though it was the battlefield between constantly warring groups of organs. Her pains were the result of the wounds and setbacks of all she had endured in the ever recurring campaigns. Which side would win, or what the result of winning would have on her, and the consciousness of her body, she had no idea; except that it would add further torment. What could she do, but seek to bring a truce in the warfare, and to pacify all the combatants by using the haphazard supply of medicines which arrived on the supply vessel? One medicine above all she valued as a pacifier, laudanum. But her husband, who had the audacity to believe that he knew what was best for her, only allowed three pint bottles per supply ship. These never lasted, never ever lasted. She was so often racked by pain and a little sip morning, noon and night worked wonders for her. It was her special medicine, but that great oaf of a husband refused her a constant supply, just as he refused her every blessed thing else.

He had never loved her. Had only loved himself and

that love affair had grown over the years until there was only him and his needs and wants. It—now she realised—had always been like that. The only reason he had married her was that she was above him, and so he had thought that by marrying her he would automatically rise to her level. That would never be and he would remain a member of the lower orders until the day he added his own grave to the others he prayed over. Why, he was little better than the poor convicts they insisted on sending out to rot in the colony. Poor things. She pitied them, but they were all rogues, male or female, and she was better off without having them around. Servants indeed. A lot of thieving rascals. Why, you had to keep an eye on them, morning, noon and night. Now she had those so-called civilised natives for servants, that Ludjee, who had been around her husband for God knows how many years until she had become civilised in conceit. At least, she did her work better than that convict lass she had had: the one who had become mysteriously pregnant and had had to be sent back to the female factory. Hussies the lot of them. Trash, just like that husband of hers with his aspirations to become a gentleman.

Become a gentleman indeed. How she used to laugh, behind his back for sure, but still laugh for all that. Him and his practising hour after hour in front of the mirror to find and keep his aitches. After years of effort, he had succeeded enough to hoodwink those in authority, but for all that, he had only managed to obtain a post on this miserable island where she languished along with him. Superintendent of the Government Mission For Aborigines, indeed! A grand sounding title for a poorly paid job, but then he wasn't up to anything else. He was so inept at numbers that she had to keep his books for him. Thank God, her daddy had been a shopkeeper and had made sure that everyone in the family could figure. If it wasn't for her father, God rest his soul, and herself, that worthless man would have stayed the bricklayer he was meant to be. Sweet Jesus, she had been such an innocent ninny to allow herself to be taken in by his sweet words. That's all he was: words. And that's all he had, never anything else, and she had allowed him to persuade her to follow him here and to live among an almost extinct tribe of savages.

And here they were, right on schedule, beginning their unearthly din in the middle of the night while she lay in constant suffering, while that great lump of a husband snored on beside her. God, those savages were melodious compared to his bestial snorting. And how healthy they were. Not a sickness among them. No, that wasn't right. The poor bastards were as badly off as she was. Dying off under the ministering hands of her inept husband. He would be the death of all of them, just as he would be the death of her. Why, when she was well enough to get around, how it hurt to see the little ones lying there so sickly. It made the heart so heavy, but perhaps they were better off away from it all. Sometimes, she thought like that. You know, getting it over once and for all. It would be better off all around. What good was medicine when that unfeeling brute of a husband rationed it out? No good at all. What he should do was give them as much laudanum as they needed. Give us as much laudanum as we need and save us good and proper. No more any of us suffering and calling and singing out our woe, our pain, our ill-health, our need to enter into a realm of health. No more of that—but a constant supply of laudanum would never be, not while that good Christian, the Bringer of Salvation was in charge. Christ, how he snored. Well, he wouldn't for long.

Savagely, the woman dug her husband in the ribs. He gave an extra loud snort and turned on his side.

The cacophony of his snores resumed. Out of tune with the natives singing outside, they angered her so much that her pain disappeared. She hit him savagely across the nose. Startled, he sat up wildly. Aghast at her action, she sought a victim and settled on the convenient victims caterwauling the night away with their pagan cries.

Both now awake, they listened as on the wind came the voice of Jangamuttuk miming out perfectly words in the very voice of her husband. She couldn't help grinning at him in the darkness.

'They made of me,
A ghost down under,
Gave me a dram,
It tasted like cram,
Real as my dream
Way, way under.'

The intent of the words rankled her and the grin turned savage. This brute, this brute beside her had lured her out from London in that smug voice. Him and his promises. 'Stop them, stop them!' she demanded of her husband.

Fada had rather enjoyed the mimicry. He took great pleasure in the natives and their simple, but effective ways. In fact, so much were they in his regard, that he was in the midst of writing the definitive text about them. Nothing would have suited him better now than to pick up his pen and jot down the rude but simple rune. It was with such amusing anecdotes that he wished to lighten the heavy brief of his volume: the taking of the message of goodwill to the poor natives of the Empire. He sighed at the greatness of his mission.

'Will you make them stop! I can't stand it. I'm not asking much of you. I have never asked much of you. Please God, just make them stop. I've had enough for one night.'

Fada sighed in annoyance. How could he have dragged this woman all the way across the ocean? How could he, when she so obviously was not a help to him in his mission, more a hindrance? 'So help me, God,' but it was so, and he sighed again.

'Well,' the demand fell between his bed and his journal.

There would be no rest this night, unless he went to quieten his charges. In many ways this could be made to work for his benefit. Why, it might prove to be the basis of an entire chapter of his volume. The thought pulled him out of bed. His wife groaned at his portly unromantic figure clad in a long nightshirt and with a nightcap pulled low over his balding head. With a deep sigh, she turned and faced the wall, waiting for him to be gone so that she could have a dose of her favourite medicine and achieve blessed sleep.

It was not in the nature of Fada to play the sneak. Thus he strode away from the mission compound and along a track (a visible fruit of his labours), in the direction from which the sound of clapsticks and digeridoos came. With a smile, he waited for the mimicking voice to begin again, but it did not. His eyes adjusted to the starlight and he walked briskly along, sensing that the music did not come from the cemetery at the end of it. A cemetery too quickly populated, he thought. The rhythm came from somewhere to the right and from the forest. Knowing that there were no dangers to be feared from savage or tame animals on the island, he confidently left the track and groped his way through the dark bush. The starlight made the scene tremble and become a romantic wilderness. Trees assumed fantastic shapes. A storm had lately come crashing through the forest. It created havoc among the giant trees. Huge boughs were ripped from the mother trunks and tossed yards away, or had just been pushed down to crack and

11

lean half-detached. It was as if a giant had charged through the bush without heeding the consequences. Fada breathed a prayer of thanks. His flock had been spared from this natural calamity.

The fallen boughs made for rough going. Fada for an instant forgot his good nature, and cursed the tricky devils who sought to hide their shenanigans deep in the forest, but his good humour at once returned. He smiled at the childlike simplicity of his charges who had so skilfully evaded his sight, but who were so unaware that the sounds of their revelry would travel to his ears. Then, through the giant boles of the forest, he saw the flickering of fires. He went forward softly and crept to the edge of a sylvan glade. There in a forest fastness, his charges, supposedly safe from his all-seeing eye, were indulging themselves in a ceremony which reminded him of the mass of the Popish Church of Rome. Fascinated, he stayed hidden in the darkness behind the illumination of the fires. His romantic nature came to the fore. He felt like some elfin spirit watching the mysterious ways of the humans.

Jangamuttuk was afraid in the realm of the ghosts. Soaked through, he huddled sodden as the ground beneath and the air around him. After, or before, now, he reached out for his *mapan* power living in the pit of his stomach. Standing, he took a long look about him. Mist and the smell of decay. In the distance, but what was distance, close, rose a hill fantastically shaped by the weather of this forbidding country. Such was his human reasoning, but then his special ghost knowledge entered his mind. It was a castle, a dwelling of the higher ghosts who would hold the medicine that would bring health to his people. He had to get inside, but as he looked, it receded from his vision. The tall foreboding walls were unbroken and mocked his fragile humanity. He needed his Dreaming companion. With longing, he

12

sang for him. Sang a song that came from his secret initiation. His clapsticks tapped out the strong rhythm. From his external initiation, the didgeridoos took up the rhythm. He let the sound lift him towards the castle walls. He sang his song again, calling, calling. He fell to earth beside the white walls hazy in the swirling mist. Rain began pelting his naked body, washing away the immunity of the painted symbols. His power began ebbing. Desperately, he clapped his sticks together. The didgeridoos roared out his urgency. Now, a familiar warm wetness passed over his head, and his clapsticks changed to a rhythm of welcome. His power flowed as he looked up at the stone axe-head of Goanna bending to accept him. Now with his special Dreaming companion, Jangamuttuk the shaman laughed as he scrambled up on its head. Now the walls were thin as paperbark to him.

The back of Goanna was ancient and even his sacred skin patterns were faded. Jangamuttuk could remember his first journey with him, then the patterns were clear and well marked. They had gone to form his most sacred body paintings, and in the old days, when culture was strong, the sight of them would have inspired fear in women and children. Now they might be identified, if at all, only as the mark of the Goanna Dreaming. Jangamuttuk lovingly traced some of the patterns. Perhaps next time he would bring along some paints and touch up the designs, though it would be difficult, for the loose skin was pitted and scarred and hung in folds. These afforded him both hand and toe holds, and he had often thought that Goanna made them for the comfort of his rider.

Now, he watched Goanna sum up the scene in two jerky head motions. He lumbered forward a few clumsy steps, gathered himself and raced up the wall. It always amazed Jangamuttuk how swift and agile his Dreaming companion was—and how sure in his knowledge. For as swiftly as he had begun, he stopped beside a narrow opening invisible from below. Pushing his clapsticks through his hair belt, Jangamuttuk squeezed through into a passageway similar to the one leading to the sacred cave where in the not so long ago, when they were in possession of their own land, the tribal bones rested. But nowhere was there the familiar feel of hard rock, or ancestral power. All along and underfoot were soft skins with the fur turned inwards. The smooth surfaces were covered in designs and figures of such mystical intent, that he wished that he had the time to draw some, but he had to hurry onwards. Testing that the power was still with him, he pulled out his clapsticks and tapped out a jaunty rhythm, a play rhythm that he had often played to the children of his community. A feeling of sadness overtook him, for gone were the times when children could dance carefree to this rhythm. The didgeridoos replied to his sadness and urged him along.

He knew that his time was limited. The atmosphere pressed on him with a sense of dis-ease that threatened him with sickness. But his need and the need of his people cancelled out the sense of foreboding. He wanted health. They wanted health. All were far too depressed to endure the island prison much longer. They were becoming tired of life. Then his need for health met an answering need. Strange scenes threatened to take over his brain. They were of such ghostly intensity that only the strong magic of his shaman nature kept him from going insane with a longing for something that was beyond all his understanding. Unsure of his power, he took on the shape of a spider and darted along a safe strand towards his goal. A slab of wood attempted to bar his way, but he passed through and found himself caught fascinated by the bloated horror that hung in the centre of the web. It had not been his web, but her web. She reeled him in. The slavering jaws fascinated. He was paralysed,

14

unable to escape . . . Then the urgency of the didgeridoos danced him free. He changed from a spider back to the shaman, then into his Goanna familiar, then back again as he found himself out of danger.

A ghost female lay on a platform covered with the softest of skins. She was fair to behold. Stark white and luminescent was her skin beneath which, pulsing blue with health, Jangamuttuk could see the richness of her blood. Her lips were of the reddest ochre and her cheeks were rosy and glowing with good health. Her firm breasts rose and fell. She slept the sleep of a being seemingly content in body and spirit, but Jangamuttuk with his insight knew that this was an illusion. A wave of ill-feeling from her nightmare shivered her form and before his eyes the fair illusion of her face twisted with a hunger which might never be satisfied. Her longing extruded from her to fix his attention on a small table within reach of her groping hand. On it stood a golden flask. The source of her good health. Before the hand could clasp it, Jangamuttuk snatched it up.

The eyes of the ghost female sprang open. Blue and utterly cold, they held him. Wrenched from a dream in which she was on the verge of finally and utterly achieving complete satisfaction, her hunger erupted in a scream of rage at the human. The female sprang at him. Before the claws could fasten on his throat, he regained his power and sprang aside. Thwarted, she glared at him, readying her body for another attack. This gave him the edge he desperately needed. Thrusting the neck of the flask through his hair belt, he lifted his clapsticks and began a pacifying rhythm. She hung, her body quivering in the urge to spring upon him. Softly, he began to chant:

'Now the darkness holds my soul,
His voice keeps me from the source,
Thunder, thunder, lightning strikes

15

Holds me still in my wretched plight.
And I groan, moan, no pain can quell,
Or hope can quench, the sorrow of my hell,
Down under, living hell down under.'

The truth of the spell safely held her. The didgeridoos swept into a petrifying rhythm while he searched for an escape.

A perfect cube held both of them prisoner. But he was threatened by more than imprisonment. The angry female struggled to free herself from the bonds of rhythm. Jangamuttuk pressed at a slap of wood marking one of the vertical sides. His ghost knowledge failed him. It was only design without function. A small square in the opposite side. Suddenly, he knew that it was the way to escape. He rushed to it. The female glared and lunged at him. The rhythm held her. He thanked his master for the gift of the chant, as he poked his head through the opening and saw, alongside, his Dreaming companion. He grabbed two handfuls of rough skin and swung himself across the broad leathery back. With a rush, he was away with the medicine safely tucked in his belt. From behind came a loud shout of rage, followed by a scream of despair . . .

Fada watched entranced as the natives acted out their travesty of the central ritual of a Popish mass. Each couple approached that rascal of a Jangamuttuk and received from what he could have sworn was one of his wife's old medicine bottles, a drop or two of seemingly precious fluid. This, indeed, would make for another amusing anecdote; but Fada was more than startled when the villain mimicked an awful travesty of his better half's voice. This was too much of an imposition, especially if she was still awake and listening. Visions of the endless barrage of words he would have to put up with for the

16

rest of the night forced him to act. Stepping into the light of the clearing, he commanded: 'Stop!'

Petrified by the apparition in the long white garment and nightcap, they instantly obeyed him. It was indeed a ghost summoned hither by the ceremony of their shaman; but he, they knew, had the power to send the apparition back whence it had come.

Jangamuttuk, feeling himself coming out of his trance, hastily said farewell to his Dreaming companion. Satisfied that he had fulfilled his task, he looked up and into the angry eyes of a ghost. He tensed, then relaxed. It was Fada, his tame spirit.

'Jangamuttuk, you old villain, you will put an end to this immediately.'

'About to boss,' Jangamuttuk smiled, humouring him.

'And did I see you with a bottle of my wife's medicine?'

Fada, without waiting for an answer, came towards the shaman. Jangamuttuk hastily stood up in case the ghost turned violent. He knew that sometimes Fada took exception to nakedness, and here he was naked except for his shell pubic ornament and his hair belt in which he had thrust his clapsticks. 'No, boss,' he replied as he hurriedly made off and out of the clearing.

The rest of the people followed him and Fada, feeling somewhat foolish, was left alone. With a mental note to himself to fix the rascal in the morning, he poked around the spot where Jangamuttuk had been, looking for evidence with which to confront the old man with thievery. Not a thing. Strange, he could have sworn . . . and not a stitch on the beggar. With a shrug he dismissed the whole incident and let his good humour return. He stared around the deserted clearing and found himself alone, romantically alone in the wilderness. How he wished for a charcoal stick and a sheet of paper. 'Deserted ceremonial ground', would make a fitting title for the sketch. Perhaps (at least he fervently wished) his wife had lapsed into a sleep, leaving him the rest of the night free to make notes on the fascinating ceremony he had witnessed. The body paintings were of such a degree of intricacy that he might not be able to reproduce them in their entirety, but then over the years he had seen enough of native ceremony and body painting to improvise on the design. But these ceremonies, they must stop, and it was his Christian duty to end them. He sighed. The missionary and the anthropologist uneasily shared his soul. The stern Christian knew that these pagan ceremonies had to go, whilst the anthropologist (and the romantic) found a natural joy in them. Was there a middle way which accepted both Christian duty and scientific enquiry? He sighed again, as he left the clearing with a last sad look.

On the way back to his house, his mood lightened as he began to plan out an interesting paper for the Journal of the Royal Anthropological Society. His last effort had elicited a number of most favourable comments from the learned gentlemen of the Society. Now he was sure that with his next publication, he would be well on the way to achieving his ambition to become a member of that august body. He smiled with satisfaction and quickened his pace . . . and to think that he had started life off as a bricklayer.

II

'It's often when in slumber I have a pleasant dream
A'lying in old Ireland beside a purling stream,
With my true love upon my side and a jug of ale in
hand,
But I wake a broken-hearted man far in this dismal
land.

'That true ghost song. Contain whole meaning of
ghosts. Learnt it from 'em way way back, when a lit'le,
lit'le fella. Just like you two 'uns. Maybe smaller, 'cause
you getting' ready to be men. That time, I was one two
year off that. Just lit'le fella, just off me mummy's tits.'
A burst of coughing interrupted Jangamuttuk's voice,
and he hawked, then spat before continuing: 'Saw 'em
when they first come from that "Ireland". One of their
homelands, 'nother one called London, then England—
maybe more 'cause there's lots and lots of ghosts. Dunno
why they not stay in their country. Too cold. When I
go there always find it too cold. Foggy, boggy—all of
those things. It far from here. So far that only clever
man, *mapan*, can go there. Anyway, they must've had
a fight, somethin' like that and had to flee. Came over
this way. Sailed by my country, then came back and
took it, just like that. No shame; but they don't think
like us. Different skin and different way. They almost
finished us off there. But us, the ones who were left,
they put us on one of their big whatchamecallits—ships
and brought us here. They try to make us like they are.
Keep us here until we are all like them.

19

'The huts that we must live in are built of sods and clay,
With dampened straw for bedding and we must not say nay.
Our cots are fenced by mist, we slumber when we may,
And I wake a broken-hearted man and sing this my lay.

'Well, when I first saw 'em, didn't know what it was.' He stopped and snapped his fingers in six directions, then went on: 'Talk about 'em, think about 'em and next thing you know they flockin' all about you, wantin' to learn your secrets. Well, this is one of 'em. Keep it in mind; that snappin' of the fingers. It keeps all the devils away. Ship—you know, I thought it was a log of wood. Big log of a tree with boughs poking up floating in the sea. Funny leaves like clouds. Caught the wind and moved it along. Lit'le ignorant fella then, not been through manhood ceremony. An' then, you know, there came this thunder sound. Not lightning though, just great big sound. Louder than the crack a bough makes as the wind hits him and snaps him clean off. Then lots of smoke. Lots and lots of smoke and I knew that it was ghost sound, 'cause Lightning man, he belongs to us, brother to our Dreaming. He would've come and showed himself, reassured me, that lit'le kid. But he didn't, and that sound and that smoke made me a bit strange, lit'le bit funny in the head, sorta changed it around so that I saw more things than was good for a lit'le kid. An' when I got back to the camp, the ol' fella knew right away that I had been gifted, that I had received my callin', my Dreamin', that Ghost Dreamin' which is so powerful when you use it right. Anyway, we better hush now, for I see a woman comin'. None of this woman's business, though maybe that Ludjee has received the Ghost Dreamin' too. Maybe, for she knows them ghosts deep down and through and through.

Listen to this song verse, you two, then hide yourselves.

*'There was a girl from Dublin Town, Rosanna was her
name
For fourteen years transported for aplaying of the game.
Our master bought her freedom and kept her in his
hand,
But she suffered deep deeper down in this dismal land.'*

The two novices, all big brown eyes and scrawny near
adolescent bodies, did not acknowledge Jangamuttuk's
comments. They were forced into silence by their coming
ordeal. Now they had to keep quiet and think over and
over what the master was saying. They had been chosen
by him to carry on the culture and they had to learn.
What with the exile of their people, few of the adult
men bothered to take care of the kids. Many had
languished and died. They might have too, except for
the *mapan* selecting them and keeping them strong for
the ceremony. They were not to go near the mission
until they became men.

Jangamuttuk still believed that the old ways could
be saved from the hands of the ghosts. Most of his people
on being exiled had fallen into despair, their minds fixed
on their faraway homelands; but while they pined, he
roamed the island seeking for the net of power that kept
the entire Earth together. There were few places of strong
power. Only a few ancient nodes that flickered in his
awareness. These he accepted as the footprints of his
Dreaming ancestors who had passed through the island.
Many places along the coast and beaches he found
overprinted with the recent remains of the ghosts. Here
a broken bottle, there a rusted hoop, a shattered barrel,
pits filled with the skeletons of butchered animals. To
protect himself as he wandered, he sang out verses from
his Ghost Dreaming cycle which seemed to fit the

topography of the island. Now all had been arranged in a song cycle which he would pass on to the novices. It would have to do until the old ancestors revealed to him a new song series.

One place which still retained traces of power was high on the hill overlooking the bay where the ghosts had deposited them, and where Fada had ordered them to stay. Stone tools and chips were cemented into the stone floor of the deep rock shelter and impressed in the back wall, and now part of the surface of the stone were the painted imprints of ancient hands. Jangamuttuk felt the power of his ancestors residing there. He chanted softly to the nascent power, feeling it stir, but it had been so long ago that it might no longer quicken.

The shelter itself was the very end of a narrow cleft cut into the broken edge of the hill slope. He made it a shrine and himself the Keeper of the Shrine. He made his camp at the mouth of the cleft. This formed a natural camp site. Long ago, a huge round boulder, a ball of the wind giants, had been tossed down to cover the top of the mouth of the cleft. It hung over the very edge and appeared ready to complete its journey down to the coastal plain. Jangamuttuk knew that only the power of the ancestors held it there. He sang softly of their action. In the Dreamtime, they had set up a camp for him, then entered the cleft to leave their essence there.

Now Jangamuttuk looked down the cleft towards the shrine and caught the inquisitive faces of the two novices peering out at him. Gruffly, he ordered them right back to the shrine. He followed this with an abrupt movement of his hand which left no room for argument. He expected instant obedience from the novices, but also some spark of fire. What use were yes-men to him and to their community? They were in seclusion and not allowed to be seen by any but initiated men. He stared down at the forested coastal plain. From this height, he could see the square ceremonial ground of the night before and nearby the double circles of the traditional ceremonial ground. He had tried to hide this as best as he could but from above it stood out. Still, it might not matter. Fada was the only threat to their secrecy, and he was as old as he was, and could not make the climb to his camp.

He tried to see the woman who was making her way to his camp, but she was in the lee of the hill and hidden. He continued staring down. His eyes flickered over the rough-hewn cemetery. So many of his people lay suffering in an alien soil. He sighed. He had tried with all his skill to help them. Had led soul after soul towards the silvery shining track snaking up to the skyland, but each had broken away to run wailing back to this island. Now, they tugged at his consciousness, and he let his mind relax. The ship tacking into the bay disappeared from his eyes. Pale, rounded souls squatted about him. They lacked mouths, but still were trying to tell him something. He concentrated. The words were whispers in his mind, garbled and in a language he might once have known, but since had forgotten. He concentrated in an effort to understand. The sea, the ocean heaved and spat at him. Old fears gripped his heart. Tradition made him flee from the ocean, made him believe it would swallow him whole. A huge snake writhed from the depths and turned, its jaws gaping at him. A huge snake that suddenly flashed with all the colours of a rainbow to turn into Dreaming companion. Goanna came up under him and sped away. He sported, diving deeply into the depths, turning and charging to leap high above the surface. Jangamuttuk clung on for dear life feeling the waters grabbing at him. Then he felt his power and relaxed. The waters flowed around him and beside him and in him. Now Goanna and the souls swam west towards the setting sun. He saw the sun writhe into the coils of the great serpent, and eyes reached out to give him an assurance that he was welcome.

The supply ship tacked into the bay. It tried to make its way towards a headland to shelter in the lee. The wind blew from the land and the ship, unable to anchor, ran out to sea. A small dot on the beach moved towards the tail of a thin white snake laying across the grass-covered sand-dunes. Its body twisted into the thick forest which covered the plain, changed colour and continued on as a red serpent with a bloated head which was the wide clearing in which the mission had been erected. There stood a line of wattle and daub huts for his people; a large low brick bungalow for Fada, his wife and two sons; a store with an office from which rations were distributed; and lastly at a short distance from the bungalow, a chapel in which Fada entertained them with incomprehensible sermons which hurt his head when he tried to reason them out. Then at the end of a short track leading inland, that poor patch planted with the corpses of his people seethed with restlessness. He sighed, distressed at the sight.

A cold feeling began at his chest and spread up into his throat. He coughed and spluttered, managed to bring up a great gob of phlegm, then lay back on his blanket. He became a sick old man as his young wife, Ludjee, stepped onto the platform of the camp and stood there getting her breath. She fanned her face with a piece of cloth, put down a basket, untucked the skirts of her shapeless ghost shift from between her legs, then took off the small cask of water she had tied on her back and poured a drink for the old man. Ludjee helped him into a sitting position to take the water, then gently scolded him: 'You feeling poorly this morning, ain't you? You an old fella always forgetting yourself and what happens. You become good for nothing.' She set down

24

the empty pannikin, sighing as she did so. 'Like most of us just good for nothings these times; but today, most of us are feelin' a little better. You really some kind of doctor, but you gotta watch out for yourself. Those ceremonies take a lot out of you. You gotta watch out for yourself. You get too sick and we all finished.'

Jangamuttuk, playing his role, weakly muttered: 'Should've kept some of that medicine in that bottle for meself.'

'You should've seen the missus this morning. Hunting high and low for it. She frantic, but she got two more and we need it bad.'

Jangamuttuk protested: 'No that medicine not the right one. Anyways that Fada, he knew I had that bottle last evening. He must've been hidin' and watchin' us. Both of 'em'll keep that medicine to themselves from now on. But never you mind, I find 'nother and better one.'

'He always watchin' us,' Ludjee agreed, then added: 'But we watchin' him too. Now, I got you some food. Good stuff, what he eats himself. Took it from right under the nose of that, of that woman of his.'

'Would like some kangaroo, just a little taste,' Jangamuttuk whispered wistfully. 'But most of all, a little bit of possum. Just a little bit. You remember, when we were getting together. You were a wild one then, just got your hair down below and scarcely broken in.'

'And you were a stodgy one. Wonder how you got your goanna to raise its head,' Ludjee replied with a laugh.

Jangamuttuk smiled as he answered: 'My Dreamin', woman. My Dreamin'.'

'Those times, they just like a dream,' the woman whispered. 'All we have left, dreams of home, that's all, dreams of home.'

Their own land was not so clogged with trees, with undergrowth, with the thickness of vegetation. Tall trees grew apart, their trunks only coming together in the shadows of the early morning or late afternoon. Grass grew in clumps and the people could walk where they wanted without having their feet torn by bindies. In fact so gentle was the earth to their feet that other communities called them: the people with soft soles.

But all this was long before the coming of the ghosts. They had arrived and everything had changed. The Earth raged with giant fires; kangaroos and wallabies began to disappear, and even the giant animals of the ocean were dragged ashore to be butchered. Their flesh was torn off their bones and flung into giant pots to be rendered down over the raging fires. The smell of boiling flesh rose with the smoke and a haze of death hung over much of their land. Such were the times, and everyone had to adapt to them. The girl Ludjee had been taken in by ghosts and used and abused as everything was used and abused. But then had come Fada with his promises to protect, and things had taken a turn for the better. This was before the time of the stolen children, and where hope bloomed so did marriage. It was only natural that after a grieving Jangamuttuk had seen his first wife safely off along the skyroad, that he felt the need for a woman. He saw young Ludjee who stood in the correct relationship to him. In fact, as men of marriageable age were scarce, her anxious father had settled the matter without asking for the customary presents. However, Jangamuttuk to show his observance of the old ways had scrupulously followed custom.

Ludjee smiled as she remembered the part she found she had to play, namely to enact the role of an innocent young thing towards the mature man who attracted rather than repelled. But it was then custom and Jangamuttuk, ever the conservative, would have thought her ill-bred if she had not gone through with it. So secure in her blooming womanhood was she, that she had taunted him with her ripening breasts and loins. She had enticed and repelled him until the full confidence of her womanhood flowed in her, and she could scoff at the aroused attraction of the person who was to be her man. So it had been and so it might never be again. On the island of exile, men and women mated hurriedly and without thought for the morrow. Why wait and follow custom when one might be dead? She sighed as she thought of Fada and the things she had to do to survive.

But then the memory of that last delicious time on their land with places still free from the influences of the ghosts removed her sadness. One morning, she had enticed (only a backwards glance was necessary now) her future mate after her. She knew where to go. Far inland towards the rugged backbone of their island was the place where, as custom demanded, all brides led their grooms. What happened there was supposed to be hidden, supposed to be part of woman's magic. Sometimes more than one man followed a woman, and then when a couple returned, no one mentioned the other suitors who were seen no more. Sometimes, even a single suitor disappeared and only the woman returned. Such things happened, and they were accepted because they made the race strong. But this time, only the male Jangamuttuk alone remained in proper relationship to her, and so the marriage was ordained.

In a valley turfed with grass and shaded by evenly spaced trees, Ludjee lured her mate. It was woman's country, and only his desire would protect him from certain destruction. She reached the pool which was part of all women's Dreaming. And Jangamuttuk, a stickler for the rules, had come to stop beside the cool waters. His eyes reflected a rainbow as he watched her. She felt

27

his eyes swarm over her body as she floated upheld by the strength of the dreaming waters. They caressed the deep brownness of her desire, outlined her breasts and made her nipples stand out like dark sweet swollen fruit. Then she felt the gaze withdraw and in her body she felt her soul withdraw a little, as the dreaming waters waited for her lover to return.

He brought the bodies of four possums which he placed gently down on the bank where lovers had camped as far back as the Dreamtime when the first female lover had been turned into a pool to eternally receive the downflowing passion of her lover. Jangamuttuk braved the water. Gingerly, he lowered himself and was swept towards the rainbow. She saw how his body glowed as it passed through the rainbow and moreover saw that he could not swim and was in danger of being taken into the depths. She swam to him and towed him into the shallows. Safely in her arms, he could resist her no longer. They merged oblivious of the dreaded present and future which was wrenching them from this past.

Jangamuttuk chanted out his memory: 'And after, we roasted those possum over the fire.'

And Ludjee chanted a reply: 'And they still are the sweetest, the most tender possums I have ever eaten . . .' Then her voice became as bitter as the salt sea: 'Now all gone. All spoilt . . . All that happiness, all that land, that Dreaming place which held us both.'

'But we still together, Ludjee,' the old man whispered. 'We still together. No matter what happened. We still goin' strong together.'

Suddenly, he broke into a fit of coughing, and Ludjee made him eat some of the salt pork she had taken from the mission house and the vegetables which she tended in a little garden of her own. It had to remain hidden, for if Fada knew, he would first commend her, but then take all the vegetables for his own table.

'You gotta take things easy, old fella,' she gently scolded him again as she watched him masticate the pork. 'Take things easy, else I lose you.'

'No, I ain't a thing to be lost. When I go I know I go. I am a boss of that world. Time come to go, I know. And not from this island either. Almost got answer I been looking for. It almost come to me now. When I get it, maybe, just maybe, I take this sickness and fling it into Fada. Maybe I just do that.'

'Not Fada, he good man,' the woman protested. 'He done his best for us.'

'Maybe his best not good enough. Maybe his value is at an end,' the old man said, flinging off his assumed weakness.

Ludjee was alarmed. She knew her husband was capable of hurting Fada and she didn't want that, though sometimes for all the world, she couldn't understand why she felt such tenderness for the ghost. Maybe, she had more than once thought he was the spirit of her grandfather come back. He had been thickheaded like Fada and clubfooted as well, though Fada was not. This kept her from making a full identification of Fada with her grandfather, though she still felt protective about him. Now she raised her voice in protest and also indignation as she realised that her husband was not as weak as he made out and had been funning her. 'What you mean?' she almost shouted. 'Don't you go pokin' fun at Fada. Don't you go plannin' to hurt him with that bone-pointin' nonsense. If it wasn't for him, where would we be? Answer me that, where would we be?'

The shaman stared down towards the mission compound. His eyes fastened on the graveyard as he muttered: 'And yet that graveyard keeps growin', and them souls keep callin' to me. I see in vision, right in front of my eyes, that sickness comes from that ghost, and when we die, he binds us to him. He writes us down

29

in that big book of his and we are trapped for ever. But I watch out, I know what he is doing, and I can free . . .'

'Old fella, you talkin' outa your sickness,' the woman said softly, feeling that the old fella had suddenly weakened. 'You runnin' aroun' in that head of yours. Listen, old man, I work in his house. I know ghost talk good. I listen to what he say to Mada, his wife. He tells her that he has plan. Soon, we all up and goin' to new land.'

The old man broke into a fit of coughing, then croaked out:

'Tell me the old, old story,
Tell me the old, old story,
Of Fada and his love.'

'You shut your mouth now. A body never knows if you sick, or lying', or funnin' or crying'. You shut your mouth now and let things be until we know.'

'Woman, you the crazy one,' the shaman shouted in exasperation. 'You know how he got us to this island, you know full well. We was the ones that told them others to put their trust in him. He was going to take us to another place free from ghosts. And when we got here, them ghosts were still over us, and worse Fada was the com-mand-ant of this mission and he cut off our hair and he made us wear those clothes and . . . '

'He done the best he could. He still tryin' his heart out.'

'An' so am I, an' I got better skills than he has.'

'Well, maybe you have,' the woman answered somewhat reluctantly. 'You do ceremony as it should be done. Fada's medicine done us no good; your medicine better for us. Most of us well now; but we still here and Fada will take us away.'

'Fada's plan is my plan,' Jangamuttuk declared. 'I

30

see it all in vision. New land and no Fada. We will go soon. I know.'

'You old fella roamin' too long in head. Sickness got you alonga balls. Squeeze the sense outa you. You not Fada . . . Now I 'member' he wants to see you. Told me to tell you to come quick smart,' she replied before realising that the shaman had been speaking from a trance which he had fallen into. The state stirred things in her. Things which Fada's teaching had put out of her mind. She smiled as she watched him return.

Jangamuttuk did not return her smile. He said: 'He wanta see me 'cause I wanta see him. I, Master of the Ghost Dreaming, and he a ghost.'

'Hush, don't talk 'bout such things in front of your woman,' Ludjee said quickly. This was a warning that the novices might be listening, for she had reached the age when things were revealed rather than concealed. Now she kept the smile on her face as she added: 'Whichever way it is, he wants to see you. You go see him bye and bye. Okay, and put your pants on. He don't want to see your thing danglin' down. We civilised now, you know.'

In the cleft the listening novices wondered why the two adults continued laughing for so long.

III

Fada sat uneasily in the commandant's bungalow. Like many ambitious persons, the getting there had been more enjoyable than the arrival. Being the superintendent (he had changed it to commandant because it had a much more authoritative ring) was a position from which to look back at the ragged child in the East End of London having to scrabble in the dirt and garbage heaps for a morsel of food. No one understood that ugly existence. The so-called gentlemen of this world turned their noses up at you, not knowing what it was like to struggle, to fight to escape from that shithole into which he had been dropped at birth. Fada had never considered the proposition that the people he had come to help, hinder and change, might try and accommodate his hidden rancour by creating a myth in which his white race were seen as ghosts, and London as a cold forbidding realm filled with so much suffering that a human could not survive in it. It was impossible for Jangamuttuk to imagine the amount of pain that went into forming the lives of ghosts, such as Fada, and correspondingly the amount of effort needed to bring such people into a state of health. Jangamuttuk was concerned only with his own people. His people had been struck by a plague from that unhealthy realm, and it was his job as a shaman to heal them, even if it meant isolating and destroying the virus.

In contrast to Jangamuttuk's community approach, Fada had opted for that of the individual. To salve the horrors of that past child's life, he fought to raise himself socially above it. His class, his community meant nothing to him. They lived in a horror from which he had escaped by fleeing to the colonies. There he had become, with a great deal of strife, what he felt was the only thing capable of redressing those young years of sordid horror. But in achieving that blessed state, he had lost something, and gained a supposedly lower middle-class wife whom he could not stand, and whom he knew he had outgrown.

Mada had caught his eye when he had been flush enough to afford some decent threads. Fada had covered his tracks so successfully that even in his thoughts he could no longer be honest. What had happened was that the young chap had caught the fancy of a toff who liked what would later be referred to as rough trade. Well, this toff, had picked up the young Cockney, and had given him a long and loving bath, in the course of which certain intimacies had been shared. This notwithstanding, the gentleman was an extremely devout Christian and saved the youth from a life of a bricklayer. It was the good Christian who created Fada even to the extent of teaching him how to read (the Bible) and then to write. Fada never forgot his benefactor, and kept up a correspondence with him until the gentleman expired. His letters were cringing examples of how he had made good and sometimes bad. On occasion, when he felt the need to alleviate his guilt, he confessed his sins to his benefactor and expected forgiveness, which was forthcoming after a stern and overlong admonition.

Fada, as much as he was able (which was a great deal), took the gentleman for his model, even to the extent of adopting his Christianity and writing style. In fact so long and earnest were the missives from the gentleman, and so much did Fada struggle through them, that he developed the same longwindedness. In one respect, he differed from his benefactor. That gentleman had never married. Unfortunately, no amount of contrition could remove the fruit of Fada's early sin, or even the occasion of the sin itself. As a consequence Mada and he clung together for better and for worse and worse, until he could hardly endure being in the same bed with her.

Mada also had the gift of falsity and over the years her origins had risen to be far above her husband's, but if the truth were known, her father was the proprietor of a pub in a very, very rough neighbourhood, who demonstrated by his foul language and physical aggression that he was the master of his territory which included his slovenly wife and sluttish daughter.

Naturally, Mada didn't consider herself sluttish. No way at all. A maid had to look after herself, else she ended up with a babe in arms and no man. So when the lad in the new clothes came in, she played standoffish and let him wait.

'What do you want?' she demanded finally.

''Alf glass of gin'll do for starters.'

'And enders too from the looks of you. Your mummy know you in a public 'ouse?'

'Does your mum?'

''Ere's your drink, pay up.'

Fada, secure in the new clothes provided for him by his Christian mentor, reacted to the airs of the scrubber and put on airs of his own. He felt in his pocket and pulled out a purse that his benefactor had given him after pressing in a new half-crown and a sixpence. Now he took out the half-crown with studied nonchalance. He felt her eyes on the coin, then he put it away and pulled out the sixpence. The tart put her hand out for it and instead of merely dropping it in, he pressed the coin firmly into her hand.

'Saucy,' Mada retorted. She held the coin up to the light ostensibly to check if it was counterfeit. She felt her breasts move with her arms and knew that he was looking. Well, nothing wrong with lookin', she reminded herself as she turned away and gave him the change from the cash drawer.

Fada watched her breasts move under the grubby fabric of her blouse and decided that maybe she was there for the taking. His new clothes brought out his natural arrogance. In the East End sex was taken as it came, especially as the girls and boys reached puberty and came on heat. He wondered how old she was. He guessed about fifteen and thought that most likely she had been pronged once or twice already. 'Your dad', he began. "Ee was the big cart'orse that broke me uncle's arm. Snapped it clean through.'

'You don't say nuthin' 'bout me dad,' she began.

'Not sayin' anythin' 'bout 'im. That uncle, 'e gets a few drinks in 'im an' he's off 'is 'ead in no time. 'It me mum more than once 'e did. And 'e did somethin' else.'

Mada glanced around the empty bar. Her mum was sleeping it off in the back, and her father had gone off to see a whore. They were well out of harm's way and so she leant on the bar, making sure that her breasts were shown to best advantage, and flirted. 'An' wot was that somethin' else?' she demanded.

'You know me mum took in laundry. Always slavin' over that hot tub. Bent all over it. Back killin' 'er; feet killin' 'er'; arms killin' 'er. Just a mass of misery. Well, that uncle he 'ad an eye on 'er. Me dad, 'e was hardly around. Well, that day, he came on me Mum bent over that washtub with her arse stickin' up in the air. And before you could say Jack Robinson. Well, 'e . . . '

"Ee did wot?' Mada demanded, her face flushed.

'Well, you know . . . '

Mada giggled. 'Don't tell, couldn't 'ave been much. I tell you 'bout me dad. You want 'nother drink? No, baby, eh? Might 'ave some milk 'round 'ere. Anyway you know that Lotty the 'Arlot, that one, she comes in 'ere. Well, one time she comes in 'ere I'm on me 'ands and knees scrubbin' the floors. In that corner, the vomit smell was awful, but me dad made me do it. Well, she came in 'ere. Didn't notice me and started skylarkin' with me dad. Then she went round the back of the bar, and disappeared. Me dad just leaned on the counter with a faraway look in 'is eyes. Well, you know what? I wanted to see what was 'appenin'. I snuck to where I could see be'ind the bar and there she was under the bar, and . . .'

'Well, wot was she doin'?'

'Not tellin' you 'till you tell me the other.'

'I can show you that.'

'An' I could show you t'other; but a girl 'as to look out for 'erself.'

'Not the way uncle done it to Ma.'

'Dunno 'bout that. Other way no 'arm can come to you either. Anyway, why we gabbin' on like this? Don't even know you from Adam.'

'An' you from Eve.'

But both were flushed and one thing led to another and that night Fada swaggered down the street and around the back. The pub was still open and going strong, but the girl's mother and father were serving and the girl was supposed to be sleeping on a heap of rags in the kitchen. She let the boy through the back door, and hurriedly they got down to it. They didn't do any of the things that had turned them on that afternoon. Instead they did what came naturally with the result that Mada soon found herself pregnant. She thus joined the majority of the girls in the East End, and perhaps would have ended up like them as a sluttish wife or on the streets, but Fada had made the mistake of sticking around for more and was cornered by the distraught girl who threatened him with her father. This was enough to scare the beJesus out of him.

Fada was then a lad of fifteen going on sixteen and he didn't know what to do. It was beyond him. All he had done was what the girl had wanted, and now he was in some way the one who had to pay. It wasn't fair. It was God's trick on him. And God gave him help in his hour of need. He went into the study of his benefactor and put on the woebegone air of the street waif he knew the man so loved. But he wasn't putting it on for fun. It was deadly serious. As soon as that big cart horse found out that his daughter was pregnant, he would be after him, and Fada's life wouldn't be worth living.

'My boy, there's a small spot on your coat, but no matter. I trust that you are feeling well.'

Just a few months ago, Fada would have rolled in the gutters giggling if someone had addressed him in such genteel tones, but that was before. Now he needed this person.

'Well, my boy. You can tell me. Remember the Lord is all forgiving.'

'Well, you know. Gor, I don't know. She was askin' for it. Wasn't my fault at all.'

'My boy, fault lies in all of us. We must confess those faults time without number until we are cleansed.'

The mention of cleansing gave the Cockney lad courage enough to make a clean breast of it. Not only this, but confession was born in his heart. Over the years in letter after letter, he would confess his peccadilloes to this person who would come to see him as a son. Even when he heard that the young rascal had gotten the daughter of a publican pregnant, he allowed himself only the slightest of shudders, before accepting the confession and promising to do all in his power to make things right. Unfortunately all in his power meant that Fada would still have to face the father and then marry the girl. It was then that his manliness gave way, and seizing a suitable opportunity when his benefactor was out, he raided the cashbox containing the proceeds of a marathon meeting to end once and for all Britain's immoral participation in the slave trade. But Fada's need was more desperate than any African slave's. If he stayed around, Mada's father would kill him, and so he lit out as fast as a coach could take him away from the smoking chimneys of London. It hurt him to say goodbye to the city. But he then thought that he would soon be back when things had been fixed up. But this was not to be.

Fada fled north until he reached the Scottish port of Leith. This seemed as far away from London as it could be possible to get, but his nerves were shot. After all he was a lad of sixteen and every burly person who waddled towards him was the dreaded publican. Fada with his ever active imagination was in desperate straits, though he still had money. At first he thought of going to Africa. This from his benefactor's conversation was at least familiar, but wandering into a sailor's bar, he sat entranced at their talk of the perils of that continent. The far south land was mentioned as being the farthest point on God's Earth. This was enough for Fada. He paid forty pounds of his stolen money for steerage passage, was happy to see that he had still ten pounds left, and then before the vessel sailed, he penned a letter to his benefactor confessing his fault and weakness and begging for forgiveness. He outlined his plans for the future, then posted the letter and boarded the ship.

As it weighed anchor, he breathed a sigh of relief. The publican could never catch him now. It was one reason why he had left off writing to his benefactor until the last. The land receded and so did his fears. In fact he bloomed aboard the vessel. In the steerage there were two women, a child and thirty-three men. It was just like the crowded East End, except that at night he had the privacy of a bunk around which he could draw a curtain.

Such were the circumstances that he might have tried a trick or two with the fingers, but decided against it. Somehow the image of his benefactor kept him away from temptation, or outright sin. In the letter he had said that he had felt that he had put sin behind him and now decided to keep to this. Among the passengers of the cabin class was a chaplain who, finding the voyage of more length than a body could stand, was amenable to lightening his days with Fada. He found the youth ready and more than able to learn. The long days passed in a flurry of alphabets and grammar lessons. On one occasion the chaplain spoke to the lad of the missionary life and how millions upon millions still did not know Christ. Fada listened with his romantic soul aglow. He too would become a missionary and save souls.

But his calling had to remain unanswered for over ten years while he consolidated himself in the colony. The veneer of gentleman which he sought to affect was difficult to maintain and he had to take up his old trade of bricklaying while waiting for the chaplain to find him a clerk's job. Unfortunately, there had been an influx of swindler convicts into the colony. Such educated gentlemen, though convicts, occupied all the clerical posts. After all one could not put them to work with their bare hands, and so Fada laid bricks, then graduated to a builder of shonky houses. But all the time he cultivated the proper people, mainly Christian gentlemen who might prove a soft touch, and then luck of luck, a new governor came to the colony. A stern righteous man not beyond making a quid or two, but for all that an excellent Christian. One morning on his rounds, he stopped his horse to speak to a slightly shabby gentleman. Their eyes met. Fada recognised a kindred spirit in mendacity. Soon, he had acquired a lowly government post as the keeper of a store from which he dispensed rations to the local indigents. And from this he had risen quickly, but surely under the patronage of the Governor to become Superintendent of the Government Mission to the Aborigines. He wished to make this post the foundation for his further elevation, or if that were not possible, to at least become eligible for a government pension which would enable him to return home in dignity, especially as his anthropological work was receiving some acclaim.

Now all this may be well; but it does not explain how Mada re-entered his life. After all, she had been just a bit of a plaything and their liaison had gone as wrong as many such encounters did in the grimy East End of London. What eventually cemented the union was the ceaseless work of the Christian gentleman. Fada's letter, sent just before he boarded a ship to the farthest colony, had made a deep impression on his mind. He felt that the youth had realised the horror of his sinfulness and had spiritually become a convict to be transported to a far-off land in order to expiate his sins. In fact so taken was he with the notion, that he made it the subject of a stirring address directed at those who considered the lower orders little better than animals, and so beyond redemption. But the Christian gentleman was into redemption and not afraid to venture into such dens of iniquity as he took Mada's home to be. He was deeply shocked to find that the young mother to be was still forced to serve behind the bar and endure the vile suggestions of the clientele. The father was brought to see reason with a small donation of five pounds.

With the vulgar little hussy in tow, the gentleman somehow felt that he hadn't received much of a deal. He hoped that his protégé would be grateful for the pains he had taken. He escorted his charge to a Mrs Haliday who instantly decided that she might as well help the girl with an education while she waited for the birth. Naturally, the gentleman was expected to pay for this education. He sighed and did so. The future helpmate of his boy must have some sort of moral instruction. The uplifting of the lower classes was becoming fashionable in the philanthropic circles of England, and so the good lady set to work with a will. She was gratified to find that the daughter of a lowly publican was an apt pupil.

In fact, all that it had needed was someone from the higher orders to be interested in her welfare and like a good little mimic, Mada flung off her East End origins and hastily began acquiring all the manners and prejudices of the middle class. The girl rose so high in her own estimation, that she bitterly resented having been betrayed into a betrothal to a street urchin who, now in his letters when he was not demanding that she come and join him, was declaring how much his prospects had altered. She didn't believe this for one moment, though she had only a hazy recollection of the boy. Pressure was applied to her by the benefactor who wished to see, or know the result of his intervention. In their talks, or rather when he came to admonish Mada, he often declared that he was willing to accompany the girl and her baby to the colonies, but alas his work kept him in London. If Mada had not been seduced into respectability, her retort would have raised the hair on the back of the gentleman's neck; but alas, she was no longer the slattern from the corner pub and had learnt to hold her tongue.

Eventually, Mrs Haliday's philanthropy ran dry. She had taken in the girl so that she might have a comfortable lying-in, but now that the baby was born, the moral thing was for her to go to the father who had expressed his willingness to be a good husband and father. And so they deposited Mada and her child on a ship and left her to bewail her lot in steerage.

You should not expect that Fada and Mada actually meditated on their lives and rued their missed opportunities. Perhaps Mada the more sensitive did, but Fada had made the best of things, though he suffered his wife badly; and Mada made the worst of things and created a past more to her liking. She had sacrificed herself to a buffoon and that was that. How she longed for London and that was that.

Now Fada derived comfort from his journal. Gentlemen wrote journals and so he wrote not one journal, but journal after journal. And so the self-styled commandant sat at the dining room table and wrote unfortunately in a hand which betrayed his lack of education, though he would be the first to admit that he was no clerk. One entry read: *There has been a general decrease in the mortality of the natives. They have ceased to haunt the forest fastnesses and have returned to stay in the native compound. But while the natives have taken a turn for the better, I have been taken poorly. I have petitioned Government for the settlement to be moved to a more salubrious climate, or better yet to the mainland where the work of civilising the natives may be carried forward more expeditiously. The supply ship was about to anchor, but contrary winds have driven her off. When she returns I shall go to inform the Governor of our plight . . .*

While Fada was writing in a full concentration, which did not make for disturbance, Mada entered the room and read the last sentence over his shoulder. It made her furious. Immediately, she launched an attack on her husband in a fast, furious voice: 'So you think you're running away from me again. That's all my marriage to you has been. Me staying home and you running here and a running there. My God, why'd you bring me to this hell hole. I'm falling apart here. I can't take it. Sickness, sickness and more sickness. My body's falling apart and all you do is sit there, and when the going gets tough—off you go. I'm not staying on. What with the natives dying off like flies, soon all that'll be here are ghosts. Just wandering ghosts hungry and pitiful. Those natives! Just about dinnertime and that Ludjee nowhere in sight. Stupid natives . . . '

Her breathlessness allowed her husband to remonstrate. 'Mada,' he began cautiously, 'think of your position. Control yourself. If you spent more time in prayer you would see things in a different light. He is always ready to intercede, to lift our burdens. Ludjee, I sent to take some food to that Jangamuttuk. He persists in staying in the bush, on that hill, and I can't just leave him there to starve. Apart from being a faithful companion, he occupies a position of influence among the natives. The last of the old chiefs in fact. In the old days he was always by my side. Then listen Mada, I too have had enough of this post. It is most isolated and unhealthy. I need to use the authority of Jangamuttuk to collect the natives together. I have drafted a petition. Now where is it? I thought that it was under the journal. Ah no, in the leaves. One moment while I finish off this entry. It is most important as a record.'

The commandant ignored his still furious wife while he wrote: *taking with me the petition duly signed (thumb printed) by all of the natives. They will be of great help as agents of civilisation among the savage tribes which still inhabit the mainland.*

Mada read the entry and hotly retorted: 'You can't mean this bunch of savages. You fling some clean rags which soon become dirty on them, report to the Governor how advanced they are becoming in civilisation, then

43

sit back and watch them die off. Some civilising . . . '

Any criticism of his work infuriated the commandant. Now feeling angry, hurt and resentful, he sought to compose himself. The woman after all was in ill-health. 'Mada,' he replied sternly, 'you forget yourself again. They attend church regularly, which is more than I can say about your good self.'

Mada hooted: 'Church, indeed! They attend the funerals of their children. Poor bastards, for that's all you've given them. Funerals!'

The commandant threw up his hands in despair: 'Enough, enough, enough. Have you no household duties?'

'You're the one to talk about duties. Anyway, I'm feeling poorly today. I need a rest.'

The commandant raised his eyebrows at the last comment. He sighed with relief as his wife left the room, then looked down at his journal, re-read the last entry and nodded in satisfaction. His good spirits returned and when Ludjee entered the room he smiled up at her as she began to lay the table and said softly: 'My wife is poorly again today. You must cook me something to eat.'

Ludjee without looking at him merely said, 'Yes, Fada' and continued to lay the table.

The commandant smiled at her again, then bent over his journal, his pen busily scrawling across the page as he wrote: *My wife has been of constant help to me. She is teaching a number of the native women household duties. Ludjee, a faithful companion and the wife of Jangamuttuk who accompanied me on my dangerous missions of reconciliation which enabled the remnants of a once proud people to be saved, is an apt pupil. It is the same Ludjee that once saved my life.*

He stopped writing and looked up at the woman who was taking up the things she had laid. Conscious of

44

his eyes, she became languid. Fada sighed and wrote: *Then she was most attractive, a veritable spirit of the jungle.*

During his great journeys through the interior of the large island lying below the continent like some cast-off fragment (when almost unaided, he located and persuaded the Aboriginal inhabitants to surrender), his constant companion had been this woman. He had been in his late thirties then and more than hot-blooded. Why, he remembered one of the females; why, he remembered them all naked as the day they were born and completely unashamed. They were so unlike Mada with her prudery and her lack of imagination when urged to cater to his needs. Well, this female was unlike his wife as a horse was a donkey. He had been walking through the jungle, far ahead of his party as usual, when he had come across her, naked and alone. She had seen him and her eyes had turned wary, but he soon had taken away her shyness with a gift of a couple of bright ribbons from his rucksack. How happy she was to have them. How happy and how ready to please. But it was rather hurried as he was anxious lest the rest of the party break through the jungle and onto the beach and catch him with his pants down. That was the problem. A person had certain needs which had to be satisfied, that needed to be satisfied if the mind was to be rendered free from disquiet. Unchristian, it might be, but this is how he saw it, and then what harm in it if these savages indulged in vice as a matter of course, though they had husbands who were as jealous as any English person. Jangamuttuk was like that with Ludjee and this meant that assignations had to be arranged.

It was jealousy which seemed to have sparked off the attack. For Ludjee had come upon them as they were finishing off, and her eyes had sparked fire. He had laughed it away, but it must have rankled, for a year later, when he was camped with the people of the woman he had had, there appeared a great deal of animosity, especially when the woman sat beside him and talked. How he enjoyed watching her, particularly her beautiful features and the smoothness of the skin over her perfect breasts. It brought back so many memories that wouldn't go away. He had hoped that during the night she would come to his tent. It was then that Ludjee had warned him of an attack. Jangamuttuk also came and told him that he had left his spear in a tree and now it was gone. He also mumbled something about sorcery, but what did it matter? He was too conscious of the promise that Meera, that was her name, had given him.

But the promise was not kept, and worse luck, the atmosphere turned evil. The men sat sharpening their spears at the embers of their fires and he lay in his tent waiting. Nothing happened during the night except the wet dream which awoke him at dawn. Meera had come to him at least in that way and perhaps the woman in spirit was more satisfying than in the flesh. He wiped his belly and naked as a savage got up to go out to relieve himself. He still half hoped that Meera would be lurking there and he could put the pleasures of dream and reality to the test. In anticipation (although it was more likely because he wanted to piddle) his penis became half-cocked. Ready for action, he had grinned to himself as he pushed the flap of the tent aside and stepped out. Instantly, he was surrounded by armed men.

Instantly, without thought, he leapt away and as naked as the day he was born, he charged through the trees towards the river. Once across it, he knew he would be safe as the men could not swim. But neither could he. A figure loomed out of the jungle at one side and he recoiled thinking that it was the end. Already, he could feel the spear penetrating his body, just as (and strangely at this moment of danger, he could not help thinking this), his penis had penetrated Meera. He thanked the Lord and even swore never to think dirty thoughts again, when he saw that it was Ludjee. Now he had his saviour.

They loped together and it was quaint how peril sometimes made a person think of other things, for he slowed down to let the woman run ahead so that he could admire the movement of her buttocks. Then at the river things threatened to go wrong again. The banks were steep and they slid down the trunk of a fallen tree to reach the water's edge. He stopped knee-deep in mud and looked back. The head of a man appeared over the edge of a bush. The face appeared to be staring straight at them, then the head withdrew. There was no time to be lost, but he could not swim. Piles of driftwood had collected against one side of the tree. Amongst the debris were two large boughs which might carry him. He thrust them into the water and hooked an arm over each. He floated helplessly there and then he thought he caught a glimpse of a smile on Ludjee's face. He must have been mistaken, for the woman was panic-stricken and wailed out that he would be drowned. It took some doing to get through to her that she should push the laden boughs across the river. He was near drowned by the time she leapt into the freezing water and did what he commanded. They were safe.

But the weather was beastly and squally. Rain lashed down and he found a dry spot under a big tree where he wished to wait it out. He was shivering violently by that time, and as they had no clothing or means to light a fire, he suggested that the best way to keep warm was to hug each other. But the woman laughed at this and sped off. He ran after her and into what could have proved his undoing. Both naked, they raced into the clearing where he had set up his base camp. The convicts who

47

accompanied him set up a catcalling, and no order could quieten them. It had meant the ruin of his expedition.

Then after their return, there had been the constant rumours about him and naked women which circulated throughout the colony. Well, he had had the last laugh, and he still could remember the bouncing buttocks of Ludjee tantalising him as he raced through the jungle.

Mada reappeared for lunch. He noticed that she was more than slightly tipsy. He frowned at the glazed condition of her eyes and scowled when she commented: 'I'm on my last bottle of medicine. Such a fine quality. It's done me the world of good. Your dinner isn't up to much; but the ship's still not in. Prepared it with my own hands. I don't like that woman touching the food.'

'Mada, thank you,' the commandant replied scornfully, then added: 'But Ludjee under your training has proved a skilful cook.'

'As skilful as you were at laying bricks, or at building houses,' his wife smiled distantly before striking out: 'Architect, indeed! Now you're the big boss of a bunch of savages on a deserted island.'

'Mada, there are times . . . '

'There are indeed.'

'Wife, you must realise that all *that* is behind me. Now I am a servant of Her Majesty's Government.'

'And we have to eat this salt junk day after day. It makes me sick. I can't bear to look at it. Let alone touch it. If you want anything else call Ludjee.'

His wife left the commandant alone to eat his food. He frowned. Such improper behaviour. Indeed, what should happen is that both his wife and himself should sit down at the table and have the native servants serve them. This would not only show the elevation of their position, but also would provide a lesson in civilised living to the natives. Now, what sort of example could they give with the constant bickering between them? He took a mouthful of the salt pork and had to agree with his wife that the stuff was abominable. Thank the Lord that soon the supply vessel would be here with the groceries he had ordered to alleviate their distress, though he wouldn't be in the position to sample much of it, as he was going back with the ship to confer with the Governor. But he had to hurry and get the natives to sign his petition. He called out for Ludjee, and she entered with the heavy-hipped way of walking she had. To think that he had never sampled those hips, no matter what the gossips had said. She had never let him get even close to what she kept between her legs. He couldn't understand it, couldn't at all, seeing that she obviously had taken some kind of interest in him since they had first met. Lord, here he was thinking of her as a civilised woman. It was difficult indeed to understand the workings of the native mind, especially that of a woman. Indeed, if he knew anything of their sexuality, the men simply took it when the urge rose. So unlike civilised behaviour, but somehow so romantic for all that. Civilisation imposed restraints which were often impossible to keep. But then what was he thinking? Such restraints were what made the British Empire great. Such restraints were derived from the teaching of his religion. They meant everything to him.

He stared coldly at the woman and asked: 'Did you find Jangamuttuk?'

'He up on that hill of his, Fada.'

'Commandant, Ludjee', he corrected. 'Com-mand-ant!'

'Com, com—he better at saying it than me. He's up on the hill, feelin' poorly, just like your missus. But he got two little boys with him, teachin' 'em.'

This was interesting, and his wife had said that the natives were not learning the arts of civilisation.

'Teaching two boys? An apt pupil is Jangamuttuk,' he exclaimed.

'He teachin' 'em our old ways. Put 'em through what he calls the new Law.'

'New Law?' he asked, puzzled. Perhaps it was their name for Christianity, after all it was the new dispensation.

'He says old Law gotta be changed now that you are here.'

Taking this to be the meaning of the woman's somewhat cryptic words, he praised her husband: 'Ah, I see. I always knew that he had the makings of a good preacher. And he is on the way to see me?'

'He sick, Fada.'

'I am sick too, Ludjee,' Fada said, conscious of a slight attack of indigestion, 'but you see me hard at work still.'

'Eatin', Fada.'

'No matter. I know that he will come. We are old comrades. And Ludjee,' he said, suddenly realising that the constriction in his loins was more than indigestion. 'I was just thinking of the old days,' he went on, his breath beginning to wheeze. 'You know you were a, a sylvan sprite in those days. Perhaps, just for old times' sake, we might go to the beach, to those rocks at the point. You were a great diver then, and maybe, maybe you'll dive for some shellfish for me. Do just like in the old days.'

'Ain't no shellfish there, Fada. No shellfish there anymore.'

IV

Fada was not to be denied his little pleasures and Ludjee was to perform for him yet again. The excuse, for Fada was one for excuses, was to sketch a primitive scene for the chapter on food gathering in his definitive work. And so, with Ludjee behind him carrying a heavy armchair, he made his way towards the base of the rocky headland on the left side of the cove which served as a small port for the mission. When they reached the beach, he was not content with setting up his seat on the sand, but needed it on the headland from the end of which Ludjee would supposedly be diving for shellfish. He believed in being as near the scene as possible; but this meant that Ludjee had to lug the ungainly object directly over the rough boulders which made up the headland. It was hard going clambering over the broken surface. What made it worse was the heavy skirt dragging at her legs and threatening at every step to trip her up. It stopped her from stepping from boulder to boulder and she had to wade through the rock pools where the slippery bottom sent her sprawling on more than one occasion. Finally, soaked through and out of breath, she thudded the chair down on the flat surface of a rock with a sigh.

But her work was not yet done. Fada had her adjust his seat to the best possible advantage. He made such a fuss that she felt like flinging the chair and him after it into the sea, and all the time the drag of that heavy wet material was imprisoning her. It was enough to make a body cry, not in pain but in anger. At last Fada was satisfied. He sat enthroned, dry and comfortable, while the woman nearby was glad that it was a sunny day. She would have liked to take off her wet dress, but she knew that Fada would become upset. She stood there waiting and watching as he opened his sketchbook, and examined his charcoal stick to see that it was sharp; finally he looked up at Ludjee and ordered the woman to divest herself of her clothing.

Ludjee knew what his flushed face could mean, but after lugging the chair and becoming soaked to the bone, she didn't care. It was just another thing wrong with the ghosts and perhaps one day they would learn to accept the human body as it was, instead of hiding it under layers of thick cloth. She had never come close to understanding the urgency with which Fada ordered human beings to cover themselves up. They seemed to have a horror about humanity which might be put down to their once being human and dark. Why, she had never seen Mada once unclothed. She was always swathed in yard upon yard of material which seemed to weigh down her gaunt body. No wonder she had grown so wasted. She had so much to support, that her strength had given out, and now she spent most of the time lying down. It was really strange, even if she did not fully accept her husband's theory that their bodies were made of solidified fog and that if they went unclothed for any length of time, they would slowly begin to evaporate. This might make sense to Jangamuttuk, for he had never felt the heavy solidity of a ghost body. Ludjee on more than one occasion had felt the hardness of a ghost body, not only pressing on her, but penetrating her as well, and it had felt as solid as her own husband's. What was different however was their colour and smell. The colour was maggot white, the colour of fog as Jangamuttuk had declared. Their skin in fact was opaque like mist and underneath veins could be seen pulsing with blood. This at least showed that they had blood, as did their cuts and wounds which ran a rich red; but it was the smell that alarmed her when she had to endure the actual pressure of their bodies. It was a sort of musty smell, a reeking of decay. And even their taste was different; rancid and bad, but now even her own people tasted like that. The stale ghost food and clothing had altered their metabolism, had made them sick and smelling of corpses.

She thought this while she struggled out of the sodden cloth woven from the hair of that animal which was kept on another island close by. As the last shreds left her body, she breathed deeply and stretched happily. What did she care that Fada was running his eyes over her breasts and buttocks, or that the flush on his face had deepened.

Fada feasted on her body, his eyes misting with memories. The first time he had seen her she had been as slim as a boy; since then her body had thickened into the body of a mature woman. He gulped as she raised her arms. Her heavy breasts flattened out on her chest. A forbidden memory of his youth on the East End of London came to him. He remembered the illustrations that some of his mates passed around while they bragged of their conquests. He thought of Mada and one conquest too many. His desire left and thinking that he had conquered temptation just as much as those mates of his had conquered a slut or two, or nil, he huskily ordered the woman to go to the very edge of the point and pose there as if she were about to dive into the ocean.

'But Fada, ' she exclaimed, 'ain't no shellfish here.'

'It does not matter. I want you to pose for me. I'll put you down on paper.'

'Capture my soul,' the woman whispered.

'But where is your net, where is your wooden chisel? It must be authentic. It must be as you once did.'

'Fada, we don't make them old things no more. All

finished now same longa fish.'

'Ludjee, you know that I have a collection of artefacts in my house. Go there, take a net and wooden chisel and come right back. Quickly now, the tide's on the turn.'

Ludjee with rebellion in her heart ceased to pose and slumped. Why did he have to spoil everything? Why couldn't she enjoy this moment without his incessant commands destroying it? She began to make her way back to the beach. At least she was joyously naked and could feel the warm breeze on her skin. But he spoilt even this. Fada instantly ordered her back and gave her a lecture on wearing clothing at all times. She was about to retort that sometimes he liked her without it, but decided that there was little point in making it an issue. So she dragged on the sodden cloth and then struggled along to the beginning of the point and to the bungalow.

Fada stared after the graceless creature struggling along from rock to rock. He smiled as he saw her slip and tumble into a pool. Such a shabby figure, he thought; then dismissed the thought as being beneath him. It was absolutely necessary to train them into civilised behaviour. How could he have them going about naked, a snare and a trap for all the men on the island? Better to have their charms covered and concealed. At least in this matter he had to remain firm. He thrust the sight of her naked body away from his mind and set himself to enjoy the pleasant afternoon on the point. He smiled the smile of a man at peace with himself and his world. On days like this, he could believe that he was living in paradise. How the golden rays of the sun flooded the island turning it into a scene of primeval beauty.

Away towards the horizon, huge clouds sailed majestically by. He amused himself in finding the shapes of animals in them. There was a dragon humped up towards the west; above floated what looked like a lizard or an iguana; there a fish, and what did that look like but the fair body of a naked English beauty. He cast his eyes down to where the sea foamed off the small flat green islands which surrounded this larger one, on which he had set up his mission. One of the other islands he had begun using to pasture the mission's flock of sheep. Even there, there had been casualties, and he nodded his head in sadness, then cheered up, for the situation had improved enough for him to send the schooner out under the command of his son to butcher some of the animals for fresh meat. He scanned the horizon, for the vessel should be well into the return voyage, but there was no sign of it. Well, it was perfect weather for sailing and with the tide on the turn, his son should have no trouble in reaching the cove by evening.

He turned his attention inland. Behind the narrow coastal plain the central spine of the island loomed with more than a suggestion of menace about it. This he put down to the gloomy forests which dominated the steep slopes in mass confusion. Indeed, it was the trackless jungle of his worst dreams. On arriving on the island with a detachment of soldiers (they had been sent to guard the working party of convicts which cleared the forest and erected the mission buildings) he had once set out to conquer the peak. He thought that the view from the summit must be wonderful and a British flag flying there would mark the whole island with the promise of superior culture and civilisation. He had set out with high hopes of reaching the summit by early afternoon. Somehow he had lost his way and pushing his way through the almost impenetrable jungle had reached a clearing overgrown with tall grass. Exhausted, he had sat down to rest and had fallen asleep. He awoke in terror, his whole body covered with leeches. Only quick thinking had saved him from death. Fortunately, he had packed a large container of salt in his lunch and so he sprinkled some of it on the blood suckers. They curled up and dropped off. Free of most of them, he blundered back the way he had come. Thankfully, it was all downhill and he managed to stagger to the compound before collapsing from loss of blood.

The incident had put all ideas of climbing the mountain out of his mind for ever. Somehow Jangamuttuk must have known of Fada's aversion when the rogue had decided to camp high up on the slope. Fada examined the slope and eyed the massive boulder which clung to the hillside. It rested on what, at least from that distance, looked like two columns of rock. He should have brought his glass to make out the details, he thought, but no matter. A thin line of smoke rose from, or near, or under the boulder. That must be the camp of that old rascal, Jangamuttuk. He would clamber up there one day and order him down into the mission. Then, he felt the itching of the leech scars over his body and shuddered. Let the old rascal stay in his camp and be drained of blood. It would serve him right.

Jangamuttuk pulled and the bark left the smooth wood in a long satisfying strip. He was making a spear. A meaningless task now, for as a weapon it was obsolete, but still he enjoyed the skill. It belonged to a tradition which went back thousands of years and he wanted to pass the craft onto the two novices. They were interested and he saw how seriously their brown eyes followed his hands, as he stripped away the bark in long slivers. The bare green wood gleamed as he held it over the fire for smoking. This not only made the shaft strong, but the heat dried out the wood. He began straightening the shaft, bending it backwards and forwards over the heat of the fire, while singing the short verses of the chant to empower the weapon. He ordered the boys to repeat

56

the words after him. When they had them smooth, he wedged the shaft between stones so that as the wood dried out, it would remain straight. He knew there was nothing worse than a bent spear. Now what point would he use? He favoured a wooden tip rather than stone which broke too easily, and then there was the non-traditional glass, which made a very pretty point indeed; but it was easily shattered and thus only to be used against enemies. The glass made a frightful wound which he did not want to inflict on anyone. He would do the point tomorrow and use wood.

A movement far below caught his eye. He recognised Fada and Ludjee. Even at this distance, he could see that his wife had removed her ghost clothing. He knew that she was about to go fishing and took the opportunity to impart to the boys more of the old law.

'You know, there is two law, not one. Two law, one law for men and one law for women. That's how it been right from beginning. Man, woman follow his and her law. Only when together, laws together. This comes from our first ancestors, and from then on, we follow it. Even now, even here, you have to keep to that law, keep up that law. You me not make that law. Made by ancestors. You know, you smell man and he smell of the earth; but you smell woman and she smell of the sea. Always been like that, right back to the beginning. In that long ago time there was no sea. Land; dusty land; dry land! Land as far as your eye could wander. No water though. Nothing to break up ground and sky. All same longa one; but that different story. No water means no trees, no plants, no nothing. Then out of that dry dusty ground came Frog. She poked her head up. Looked around. No water. So she began hopping. Hopping this way, in that direction and this direction. No water. Too dry and dusty, her skin began cracking. No water. Gotta have water, you know, or nothing will grow. That's what Frog

57

thought. Gotta have water, or I can't live here. And she began to vomit up water. Lots and lots of water. It was like a waterfall coming down outa that frog's mouth. Finally, too much water came. Everywhere water. No hills or high places then, and it spread and spread. It was then that our ancestors piled up the hills and made low places for that water to run to; but all same, many men died in that water. Many men died all over. Too many men and it scared us. Some wanted to kill that Frog; but she too big for us to get at. Too big, so she not drowned in that water. She loved that water. Flew through it like a bird. Changed her shape so that she could move better. So much water, didn't need legs then. And the women, they came to her. Got on her back, saved themselves that way—well, many men drowned, but women, they belonged to that Frog ancestor. She showed them how to move through the water as she did. Now they have that knowledge. They can swim, go through the water: creek water, pool water, sea water. Go down over their head, go way down, but we men we don't belong to that Frog Dreaming, and it not our law. Can't break that law; but we can go alonga water in canoe. Turtle Dreaming, he belongs to us, comes on land to lay his eggs and have his young'uns there. So we can build canoes and skim across the water just like we were in his shell. Still, you have to be very very careful: real careful. Now, you two, just look down there. There's Ludjee and she about to go in water. She going into that water, going to find shellfish. Long time since we had shellfish. She'll be led to some by and by. Maybe we better get on down and have a feed, eh? You two come along, but keep outa sight. No one see you, let alone hear you, eh!'

Ludjee ignored Fada when she returned with the net bag and wooden chisel. She went directly to the very

58

tip of the point, slipped out of her heavy dress, spread it over a rock to dry out, and then stood there on the highest rock. Fada's eyes clung to her form and his hand began quickly sketching. She stood there unconscious of the ghost just a few yards away. She waited. The old ways began flowing through her. A connection was made and a line established. Her eyes lifted beyond the busily sketching Fada to were her husband sat with the two novices. He was a wily one and had picked the perfect camp site to keep the whole area under observation. She almost could hear his voice telling the novices those parts of the Female Dreaming which were allowed to males. She knew that he would expect shellfish from her; but there were no longer any in these waters, just as there were no possums or kangaroos on the land. The ghosts had seen to that. The female power surged within her; ancestors were connected in an unbroken line. The grid of the Female Dreaming flowed with energy. She dived into the water in a quick flowing motion which took her under and under. Fada frowned in annoyance, but she was beyond his control. She was free in her tradition.

Deep down and away from the cursed land of the island she felt herself expanding to become as wide as the ocean and as terrible as its battering waves. This was true woman's country and women alone could make the connection. Men and ghosts needed boats and ships; but all she needed was the strength of her body and her connection to her Dreaming. Her arms were fins; her legs a tail; her lungs gills. She surfaced. Her head bobbed up and down in the waves, and she felt the pain of the unfiltered air as she took a deep breath. Then with a quiver she descended down, down, down, and along the barren rocks. They had been scraped clean of all life. She left the side of the headland and swam out to sea moving close to the sandy bottom.

A grey section rose to touch her and in her surprise

she emitted a bubble of air, then smiled and relaxed. Her Dreaming companion, Manta Ray gently nudged her with her back. They had missed each other. Now they were together again and she settled onto the back of her companion, grabbing hold of the edges of her wings to cling on as Manta Ray charged off. What had taken her away from this power and this companion? The ghosts had sung her, made her lose her Dreaming and languish in misery, her femininity imprisoned in the dreary ghost cloth which hindered all movement and action. Now she was free of it. Free—and the ray broke the surface of the water and flew into the air.

Jangamuttuk saw Ludjee and her Dreaming companion with his shaman vision. It evoked powerful memories of their secret times together when, both astride their Dreaming companions, they would fly side by side, or glide on the wind. He wished to follow her, but could not as it was not the right time. These were secrets known only to the initiated and the novices were all eyes and ears when it came to knowledge. First they had to be made men and then as men they had to earn that initiation step by step.

Fada, immersed in his own collecting of knowledge, saw nothing. He had frowned when the woman had deserted her pose to dive into the ocean. Now he was intent on sketching the memory of her form. Swiftly, he sketched in the heavy breasts, hesitated over the groin and left it bare and sexless. More often than not, no, always, the dictates of polite behaviour and decorum had to be observed in illustration as well as words. He was illustrating an anthropological text and not the sort of pornography which was sold on the streets of London. He moved away from that train of thought and continued on with the sketch, little realising that unconscious memories had taken over his illustration. He was attempting to reconstitute the smudged print of a naked woman that one of his mates had passed over to him with a snigger. Thus it was that he found trouble with the way the net bag had draped over her shoulder and how she clenched the wooden chisel between her teeth before diving into the sea. He sighed. He would set these to rights when she returned, but he worked on, placing the folds of the net demurely over the breasts and moving the hand to hold the chisel over the private parts. He was satisfied with his work. Still the woman had not returned, although it was some time since she had dived into the sea. He pulled out his watch and consulted it. Ten minutes; but she was a great swimmer and must have allowed herself to be swept towards the other headland as she had said that there were no shellfish here.

Ludjee felt the strong body of Manta Ray ripple beneath her. Gently, she detached one hand to stroke her head as she lazily drifted above the mission compound. Then she had to grab hold fast as her companion banked to take evasive action as a weird bird she had never imagined before swept up on great pinions from the direction of Fada's bungalow. She (Ludjee knew that it was female), hissed hideously through a gaping red beak thrusting forth from a long extended neck. Great white wings flapped noisily, the beak gaped and hissed. Faster than the ray, she rushed around and around trying to drive them away. Ludjee nudged her companion to be gentle. She had no desire to tackle the giant bird. There was something pathetic about it. Something that was not quite right. She dipped and swung around them, but there was no real viciousness in her attacks. In fact, they were feigned, a strategy to scare them away from her nest, for far below where Fada's bungalow should have been, Ludjee could make out what appeared to be a great mound of down in which a pale naked form squawked helplessly. The sound was so pathetic that it drove into her heart. Such a sad, sad cry and then her companion rushed away from the hissing bird and that hapless form below.

They flashed across the island and descended towards a long smudge of land on the horizon. Now they entered the sea without as much as a splash. The ray swept towards a headland and drifted along its side. Ludjee saw that rocks were covered with succulent shellfish. Her companion stopped beside the rock face, lazily flapping its wings to keep in position. Ludjee prised the shell fish off. When her bag was bulging, she nudged the ray who gave a powerful flap which sent them skimming through the water. As they sped south, Ludjee felt her mood shift towards depression. She was returning to the island prison; but what else could she do?

Fada had finished a sketch of the cove and still Ludjee had not reappeared. At first, her absence made him angry and then alarmed. She had been gone for over an hour and while pornographic visions of her naked body floated in front of his eyes, he recalled she had been his sable companion for many years. Both she and her husband had accompanied him on his journeys of exploration. But never had he taken full advantage of her, though there had been opportunity enough. He glanced down at his disguised sketch of a naked English prostitute and imagined how idyllic it had once been. Then he remembered her careful nursing of him when he had come down with fever. Why, she had even decorated his crude shelter with flowers she had gathered in the forest. Such a creature of the wilds and she surely must have loved him. Now, now it was perhaps too late. A sentimental tear escaped from his right eye as he contemplated her drowned. A noble savage companion she might have been, who could have . . . but Fada cut short his musings and turned his attention onto Jangamuttuk hobbling over the beach. Hurriedly, Fada left his comfortable chair and scrambled over the rocks to him.

On reaching him, he gathered his breath and ordered: 'My chair is still out on the rocks and the tide is coming in. Bring it to me.'

The old rascal needed putting in his place, thought Fada and this was his way of doing it. But the old rascal suddenly gasped, slumped onto the beach and fell into a coughing fit. In his ill-fitting clothing, he looked a very sick old man and immediately, Fada was all concern. 'Jangamuttuk, Jangamuttuk, this no good, no good at all. I have built a nice home for you in the mission compound and yet you persist in living in the bush up on that mountain of yours. You must remain close to me. You need medicine.'

'Medicine, medicine, got strong medicine: bush medicine. Don't worry 'bout me, be right by and by,' the old man groaned and broke into another fit of coughing.

Fada lifted his voice above the racket, and tried firmness: 'Not on that cold dismal hillside. Jangamuttuk, I must put my foot down. You absolutely . . . '

He stopped as Ludjee's head rose above the edge of the headland. This was followed by her breasts, her waist, her hips. She reached down and pulled up her heavy bag. Fada was entranced. Such a primal scene. If only there was some way of capturing it for research. His sketch did not quite do it justice. Not quite, but he *had* captured the finer points of this woman posed on the very edge of the rampant ocean. He examined his sketch with an approving eye as Jangamuttuk began a new fit of coughing in an effort to shift Fada's attention back on himself. He gave up as the ghost continued to watch

Ludjee lugging her full bag to where she had spread out her dress. Fada gave an audible sigh as the woman pulled it on. He smiled as she heaved up his chair (she knew that sooner or later he would command her to get it) and dragged her burden over the rocks and through the rock pools to the beach.

Fada watched her dump his chair down, then mildly began to chastise her. He exclaimed: 'Ludjee, what took you so long? I thought, I, never mind, you're just as bad as Jangamuttuk. You should never ever go off like that.'

He turned to Jangamuttuk who had given up his fits of coughing. The two novices, none too well concealed in the undergrowth, pushed out their heads in their eagerness to see everything. Jangamuttuk had just finished signalling them to hide themselves, when he found himself the centre of attention again. Ludjee rushed to the defence of her husband and said: 'He been poorly, Fada. He old man. Needs to take it easy. Look, I got shellfish for him. They build up his strength.'

Fada looked at her bulging bag in surprise and stuttered: 'Shellfish, shellfish, I thought that there was none available on these rocks.'

Ludjee covered up her mistake quickly and exclaimed: 'Had to go a long ways Fada, a long ways.'

Fada rolled his eyes up at the duplicity of the natives. It was just one thing after another with them. They were worse than children, and just as bad as Mada. He sighed and said: 'How often have I told you, Ludjee, to call me commandant, not Fada. Commandant is my new name. Fada is so unseemly.'

Jangamuttuk broke in with: 'Yes, com-mand-ment; but she done returned with her bag filled. First time this happened on this island. Maybe things are getting better and 'em fishes have returned, or Ludjee all time great swimmer.'

The commandant sighed and made a last attempt. 'Com-mand-ant, not com-mand-ment, Jangamuttuk.'

'You good to us Fada,' Ludjee said to swing the conversation away from the word. She was sick and tired of it. 'I bring shellfish for both of yous,' she finished off with.

'Yes,' the commandant replied, but his mind was still on the shaman, and he didn't like the old man high on the hillslope. Perhaps Ludjee could help and he said: 'But, but, in short, Jangamuttuk must return to the mission compound. That cough of his . . .

'Too many ghosts, all time 'round,' Jangamuttuk answered, then added: 'Too many com-mand-ments too.'

'Custom, Fada, like you writing 'bout on paper,' Ludjee replied to stop Fada from thinking over her husband's answer. 'Too many people die all 'round here.'

Her words brought out the anthropologist in the commandant and he had to agree. 'Yes, yes, I know that this is a bad place and that it is your custom to move once a person has died, but now, at the moment, it is not, not possible. Believe me, place bad for me too. Place very bad for me, but I have to stay here alonga you fellows. I sacrifice much to help you mob.'

'You good to us, Fada,' the woman said as if this finished the topic.

But Jangamuttuk had to have the last word and he said mockingly: 'Too good to be true, com-mand-ment.'

This riled the commandant and he had recourse to a weapon he had often used. 'Very good, Jangamuttuk, and if not for me, bad person take over, one with gun, you understand, I talk true now.'

Ludjee agreed: 'You talk true, Fada.'

And so, apparently did Jangamuttuk. 'Straight talk, com-mand-ment,' he said.

'Com-mand-ant. Com-mand-ant! Jangamuttuk,' the exasperated commandant almost shouted.

This failed to daunt the shaman who again appeared to agree. 'Yes, Fada,' he replied. 'Com-mand-ant is one who com-mands and so I call com-mand-ment, just like you tell us in church.'

The commandant could not but see the wisdom in the reply. It did show that the natives were becoming civilised. 'Very good, Jangamuttuk, very good,' he commended before having second thoughts and returning to the shaman's absence from the mission compound. 'But in that camp of yours, you are too far away to come to church.'

'A commandment, com-mand-ant?' queried the man.

Again the commandant became upset. 'Oh, listen I tell you this for your own good. I talk straight now. You two fellows listen, savvy?' he stated, lapsing into a variant of native English.

Jangamuttuk was not to be deterred. 'Sickness comes from that church . . . ' he began.

The commandant shouted: 'You fellow listen me!'

To which Ludjee replied: 'You good to us, Fada.'

The commandant agreed: 'Very good, and yet, and yet, you persist in your perverted ways.'

'For your paper, Fada, for your paper,' Ludjee replied to the anthropologist.

The commandant hesitated as the anthropologist took over. At a loss for words, all he could say was, 'Well, well.'

Jangamuttuk began an offensive. 'Our ways, good, com-mand-ant,' he told him. 'Take time to change 'em, you know. Too much sickness down here. Up there air fresh. Bit cold at night though.'

The Commandant seized on this to return to the previous topic. 'There, that place no good for you. Give you cough; give you fever.'

'He 'as to be with those two young'uns, Fada,' Ludjee answered for Jangamuttuk.

'No good for those boys either. I make school for them, teach 'em proper. They learn to read and write paper same alonga me.'

Jangamuttuk was getting tired of the whole conversation. 'Good at writing, commandant; not good at doing. Many of us die here.'

The commandant then swung his words to his own advantage. 'Yes, Jangamuttuk,' he said almost gleefully. 'Yes, and that is why I need you, Jangamuttuk. You know that paper tell 'em story. I send to Governor. He reads it and sends things. Many things. Good things that you all like. Now I write important story on paper. Strong story to get you all away from this island. Island not good for you, not good for me. We go better place. Need you all to sign, to make mark on paper. You me talk to Governor and he listen to you and take you off this island. I take paper to Governor and he listen well. That way paper strong. He listen, take us all away.'

Jangamuttuk refused to concede defeat and answered: 'Maybe, maybe not. Why not we just get in boat and go?'

This set off a train of images in the mind of the commandant. He saw the natives escaping. Quickly, he said: 'No, no, no—you are safe here. You go other place, bad white fella kill you. I save you, bring you here, take you another place, but need Governor say so.'

He was grateful for Ludjee coming to his aid. She had always been there when he needed her. He listened as she said: 'You listen to Fada. He bin with us long time now. He knows what is good for us.'

Jangamuttuk smiled as he commented: 'And long time since I had shellfish. Long time since boys have seafood.' Then he changed the subject and exclaimed: 'Lo, Wadawaka comes, com-mand-ant. He takes some of us black fellas in that ship to learn her ways.'

The commandant queried: 'My son?' He looked up

and towards the far headland. A schooner under sail was tacking about it. 'Wadawaka, eh, you call my son that, eh?' he asked.

'No, that black man, same alonga us,' replied the shaman.

This set the commandant off. He was the one and only saviour of the natives, and he and he only picked the subjects to help him in his noble mission. Of course, he had picked the man to give instruction in seamanship; but that was all. 'That African convict, eh? That rebel from the West Indies. It is my son who is in charge of the schooner, not him.'

Ludjee intoned: 'Sonny in charge, Fada.'

At least one person supported him in his work. 'Yes. I must have a word with that black. I can't have him interfering in my mission. Can't have that. Why, I'll expel him from the island.'

Another voice came to support his decision. 'You tell im, com-mand-ment. He be here by and by. Enough time to go and give my boys a feed. You come Ludjee, Fada want to draw picture of ship entering cove. Be back just little while.'

V

The sun was drifting towards the horizon spraying the clouds with streaks of blood. The bottoms of the huge clouds passing over the sky turned increasingly scarlet; but their towering peaks were bathed in gold. The coiled serpent of the sun hissed and struggled to roam free above cloud and ocean; but slowly it was drawn down towards its hole in the ground far beyond the horizon. It sank lower and lower. Soon the serpent felt the first drowsiness of the night flow through its body and it rested briefly on the platform beside its hole, as it was the height of summer and the approaching evening would be soft and luminous for many hours. At last the sun began moving down into its hole and as it did so, seemingly from the serpent itself came a long trumpet blast followed by two rising short notes. The long blast from a ram's horn trumpet came again, then the bowsprit of a ship poked its nose around the right edge of the headland. It was followed by the huge bulging of red sails and a schooner swung round the rocky point, hesitated and shuddered as the wind left all her sails, then took off straight towards the land as the stiff sea breeze caught her again.

Fada had spent many sheets of paper and countless words arguing with the Governor of the colony for a suitable vessel for the mission. Delay followed delay. They had a whale boat but it disappeared one night and no one knew where it had gone. Then, on one of his frequent trips to the mainland, Fada saw a schooner which had been confiscated from a suspected villain. He organised the loan of it from the Governor, and with a convict crew sailed her back to the island where he placed her under the command of his son. He kept on one of the convicts, who was an expert seaman, to assist Sonny in teaching the natives how to handle such a large vessel (though it was no square-rigger and a crew of six could handle her easily). Now in trepidation, he watched his vessel dashing towards the land. As it came closer, he could make out the sound of the crew's voices singing:

'A is for the anchor which lies at our bow,
B is for the bowsprit an' the jibs all low,
Oh! C is for the caps'n we all run round,
D is for the davits to lower the boat down.'

The vessel scudded directly at him. He would remonstrate with his son about this. Suddenly, the sails came down all together, as another verse of the song began:

'I is for the eyebolt—no good for the feet,
J is for the jib boys, stand by the lee sheet,
Oh! K is for the knightsheads where the shantyman
stands,
L is for the leeside hard found by new hands.'

With bare masts the vessel glided towards the beach. Fada's anxiety had abated and he was now appreciative of his son's efforts. He always enjoyed a ship under full sail and his son had raced her along with dash and authority. It appeared to him that Sonny had mastered the arts of seamanship and in future days might become the captain of his own barque. The anchor splashed into the water, and the boat towed astern was drawn to the side of the ship. A dark figure clambered into it to receive the sheep carcases. When they had been stowed midships, the remaining members of the crew descended into the boat. Fada noticed with pride that his son was the last one to leave the vessel. He would be checking to see that everything was shipshape before abandoning the schooner, so as to speak. His son must have seen him standing on the beach, for the lively air of the sea shanty continued into another verse as the boat began pulling towards shore. A large black man held the stern steering oar and led the singing. This was the duty of his son, but there he was, handling one of the oars just like a crew member. He would have a word about this at once. The structure of society must be maintained at all costs. It was like a ladder with each class having its own rung. Divinely ordered, it had stood the test of time, and only those with endurance and fortitude might aspire to ascend to the next rung. Few ever would ascend to the roof where her Imperial Majesty sat majestically enthroned. Fada breathed out a long breath deeply conscious of being part of that marvellous whole.

'Q is for the quadrant—directing us near,
R is for the rudder to help us to steer,
Oh! S is for the sheerpole which we'll never climb,
T is for the topmen, far too high every time.'

The native crew ran the boat expertly through the surf. As soon as it touched bottom, they leapt out and heaved it onto the beach. Then they began unloading the sheep carcases. Fada approached his son who had one of them slung over a shoulder. He waited until he had divested himself of the load and took him aside, discreetly out of the hearing of the natives.

He began deceptively: 'Sonny, when you accompanied me on my last journey of reconciliation, you often took the steering oar of our boat.'

'Yeah, but that was then. Now whoever wants that job can have it. I like pulling on an oar. It's good being part of a team.'

'Sonny, think and consider, you are not living together with the natives in the wilderness. You are my son and are here to lead them by example and precept. Why,

71

just think, if they observe you sharing their tasks, they will lose all respect for you. I know these natives and the workings of their minds. At all times you must keep your distance. I shall not calumniate them with the charge of treachery because they are exceedingly trustworthy on occasions, as you may attest. But you are a teacher to them and must maintain the necessary distance between master and pupil. You are an apt teacher. I commend you on the sea shanty you taught them. I must put it in my report. It is a simple and effective way of getting the alphabet fixed in their memory. Why, I remember their faltering attempts in the school, while that convict schoolmaster was alive. I have written to the Government requesting another, but it will take time. Perhaps you could take up the burden until another comes.'

'Sir, it was Wadawaka taught 'em.'

'Wadawaka, who is Wadawaka?'

'The African black, sir.'

'The black *convict,* sir, and don't forget it. I might have promised him that, for his services to the mission, I would recommend that he be granted his ticket-of-leave; but that is far in the future, and I find promises are better inducements than the lash. But we are grossly undermanned here and cannot afford to take chances. Remember that, Sonny; remember how few we are. Keep a watch on him, talk to him cautiously. Make him aware of his position and how I hold his freedom in the ink of my pen. Now see to it that the natives take those sheep carcases directly to the storehouse. Here is the key. Return it as soon as they are all deposited inside. Have you made a count of the carcases? It is not beyond the natives to pilfer.'

'Wadawaka did, Fada.'

'Sonny, you have been too long among the natives; but I feel that things are about to change. Soon, this island will see the last of us. Perhaps we might even return to England. You would like that, wouldn't you?'

Sonny writhed nervously under his father's gaze. Somehow his father always made him feel like a small boy. And always, he had to answer, had to find words and more words. What could his answer be to the question? He knew a nod would not suffice. It would only bring on more words. Suddenly he switched into the spiel of his father: 'Sir,' he began, 'I f—feel that my mission is here, to help these poor heathens to see the light. Although I might like to see the home country, I know that duty bids me to stay here.' There, put that answer up your pipe and smoke it, he thought triumphantly.

Fada smiled; he had managed in this wilderness to bring up his son correctly: 'Sir, after years in the field a short leave might be managed. Now as to your duties, they are Christian and Christianity bids that you attend church. Church is where we share our fellowship with our charges, not in labouring tasks. When we all come together in His name, then He is with us. That chapel was the first building erected on the island. We all lived under canvas while it was built, then it gave us shelter while the rest of the mission was constructed. It provides us with the strength and refuge to continue on in this terrible wilderness. All, and I repeat all, must attend evening services. It is part of your Christian duty to see that they do. Together, in fellowship, we shall share the good word. And, sir, a further matter, when you must command the natives, first pass on the command to the African and let him do the actual ordering. In this way we shall establish an example of the proper order of command; not only this, but it will serve to divide them from him, for none of them likes being ordered overmuch.'

'Savvy,' his son answered, using the word to signify

disagreement with his father's duplicity.

'Sir, I refuse to see that as insolence. Now get about your business.'

With alacrity, Sonny removed himself from his father's presence, but he was overconscious of his eyes on him. Damn him and his eyes. Still, he could not bring himself to command Wadawaka to order the natives. The man was more than his equal and had taught him how to handle the schooner; besides the natives were already carrying the carcases towards the mission. He hurried after them to unlock the store door, while Wadawaka, after glancing up at him, remained behind to securely fasten the boat in case the weather broke up. In these waters a squall erupted in a matter of minutes and he had no wish to lose the boat, or find it adrift after listening to Sonny tell him about the fracas he had had with his father when the whale boat had disappeared. At least some good had come out of that occurrence as he had been assigned to the crew that sailed the schooner (and a fine vessel she was too) to the mission, and then had been ordered to stay on to teach the natives (and Sonny) how to handle her. Well, he had taught 'em and they were getting to be as smart about this particular craft as he was himself. He checked his work, for he was a methodical man, then bent down to get his shirt from the boat. He straightened up to find Fada standing next to him, though not too near.

Somehow the physical presence of the black man made Fada nervous enough to bluster. He was aware of it and could never understand why. He had been, while exiled in the farthest colony, a staunch supporter of the Anti-Slavery League. Still, there was that feeling which made him hesitate in dealing with this black man, who seemed to lack the simple faith his sable brethren had in him. Still, the black man before him was not only an ex-slave, but an ex-rebel and a convict, and had to be treated

74

with stern authority. 'Sir, sir,' he blustered, 'I find it preposterous and presumptuous of you . . . '

Wadawaka looked puzzled. He hadn't the remotest idea what he had done. He was about to shrug, but the memory of other guards using it as the basis of a charge of dumb insolence made him cautious. For a long time now he had found himself in disagreement with the likes of this self-styled commandant missionary, though it was not in his interest to be openly antagonistic. He had been through the fire and had seen more than these so fine gentlemen would see in a lifetime, though this one was a mite different: he wasn't even the gentleman he seemed! Wadawaka didn't want to go back to that other island where they were at him day after day, night after night. Just by being away from all those white folks with their constant commands had changed him for the better. He looked at the commandant without expression while his soul smiled.

'I won't have insolence, sir. That I won't. Take care, I have your future in the ink of my pen.'

It was true, and a suddenly apprehensive Wadawaka bowed his head as if awaiting punishment. These buckras never needed an excuse to use the lash and this buckra for all his religion and concern, was a buckra for all that.

Fada was beside himself with rage; a rage which had risen to flood his being. He blamed the black man standing in front of him for his anger, but if the truth were known this man had had little to do with that emotion, which was the result of thwarted lust. For the purpose of his little sketching expedition to the beach was to get Ludjee in the position where he could take advantage of her. In fact even the lugging of the chair entered into his plans, for the carrying of it meant that the woman would be too tired to struggle as she sometimes had; but all the plan for the satisfying of his fancies which had grown over weeks of abstention had come to nought, when the woman had dived into the ocean and left him alone. Now it shook his body as he scowled at the miscreant before him. This, this rebel, he spluttered in his mind, might, for all he knew, be the cunning leader of the uprising which had threatened civilised culture and order in the Caribbean. For all his obsequiousness he was a dangerous threat to the stability of his noble experiment of bringing civilisation and Christianity to his sable friends on this island where they were safe from all disrupting forces. He sternly examined the ex-slave and tried to find the evil mind of a rebel bent on destruction and mayhem beneath the pleasant face striving to remain fixed in an absolute lack of expression.

Fada's rages were short-lived and now as his emotions cooled, his Christian reasoning asserted itself with such effect that he strove in vain to find his train of thought. Why and for what had he been on the verge of shouting at this fellow and thus undermining the stern right-eousness of his own authority? Then, the anthropologist replaced the missionary and he stared with amazement at the tribal markings, the cicatrices of adulthood on the African's chest, which were exactly the same as those of his own native community. Instantly, the outlines of a paper presented itself in headings, sub-headings, paragraphs and even a few sentences in his mind. Eagerly, he inscribed the treasured paper on his memory as he began to initiate an investigation which might prove a discovery of world importance.

'Sir,' he began carefully so as not to alarm Wadawaka, 'those markings on your chest. There appears to be no mention or description of them in your personal identi-fication record. Sir, if I may say so, they bear an uncanny resemblance to the markings our own natives have on their chests and shoulders. Never in my wildest imagination did I believe that there existed a connection between this remote colony and Africa. Impossible, but it must be so, for I find it improbable that a man such as yourself who has had the benefits of the civilising process should revert to the darkest savagery of which these poor souls are still in thrall. Sir, I am well aware that Africa has been the cradle of ancient cultures.'

Wadawaka's effort to remain completely on guard fell apart. He wondered what this devil was talking about. He almost shouted 'Benin' before falling into a bitter mood. What was Africa to him, but the memories of his wretched mammy? Such a life she had had, and this person had the unreasonableness to mention Africa to him. He indeed was Wadawaka, which translated out as: Born on the Waters. He was without land, without hope, as he drifted along on the whims of the white devils, with only the sorrow of his mother keeping him wholesome, with only his rancour to give direction.

Overwhelmed by grief and anger, he broke the silence of the discipline prison had forced on him and said, 'My mammy lay naked'; then fell into an uneasy silence broken by the eternal waters of his birth. They washed against the wooden sides of the vessel anchored in the cove, and the slap, slap of the water echoed the slap, slap of waters against the wooden sides of the slaver holding his mother, soon to be delivered of her baby— him, Born on the Waters—trapped fast in the hold of her belly.

'They laid us out like salted herrings in a barrel,' he said, and then recalled his mammy's memories.

Only in calm weather did they remove the tarpaulin from the grating. Light smouldered through to touch the lucky ones lying, or huddled near the opened hatch. In the overweening foulness, his mother crouched in a far corner surrounded by the other women, who erected a wall of warm flesh around the mother to be. Beautiful and in the prime of womanhood, she was protected only by the heavy weight of her belly and those surrounding women. They would sacrifice their own bodies to the attentions of the sea serpents, cannibals, and devils, so that they at least could breathe the sweetness of the ocean air while enduring what was to be forever their lot. And when her time came, those same women who had cursed their rapers, ministered to her in the cramped conditions, with only warm hands, a container of salty water and a damp rag to soothe the agony of a first delivery. It was a wonder that a baby could survive such a birth, and the hell he found after such a birth.

For a baby was as rare as a pregnant woman on the slavers. They were too much trouble and botheration. It was easier to leave the woman behind in the equally stinking dungeons of the shore stations. But his mother had preferred the unknown to the known. Pestilence and fever and the death of her baby were certain in the dungeon in which the captives were held; but on the ocean he might have a chance. She had chosen this option and rightly so. The solid mateship of the other women had ensured it. In their dreams, they felt this little black baby in their own bellies. Sweetest of all to them was that it had been conceived by a black woman in the sunshine of her freedom by a strong black lover who had been careful though careless; but who could blame him for that? She had conceived in spite of her family and set up a home with her lover in spite of her family; then as if in vengeance, had come the arrival of the white devils, followed by the iron collar of the coffle tugging her to a dungeon and then to the stinking hold of the ship. And through all of it she had floated as if protected, as if her pregnancy was a shield against rape, and finally floating over the depths of the waters, her child had come forth; and the women rejoiced and nurtured and hid the little one from the white devils who would have eaten him, or flung him overboard with a curse.

And that had been his birth.

'I was born on the ocean,' he replied to the white devil as if this settled the matter.

Fada began to falter. Somehow the subject had escaped his control just when he was on the verge of a great discovery. He needed this person to have been born in Africa for the marks to be the initiating cicatrices of the tribal savage. His mouth hung open as he considered alternatives such as the survival of the remnants of tribal cultures among the slaves, or ex-slaves shipped to the Caribbean. He clamped his jaws together angrily as Ludjee and Jangamuttuk came onto the beach. The couple's appearance caused a surge of jealousy in Fada which he had to repress instantly. With admirable fortitude he did so; but as before, the resurgence of rectitude caused a memory loss which puzzled him. His paper was wiped from his mind as he struggled to remember why he had detained the black man.

Jangamuttuk looked back at the undergrowth growing indistinct in the twilight. He scowled as he made out the heads of the novices and gestured. They ducked out of sight, then instantly reappeared as the shaman turned away. Truth to tell, they were getting tired of not only having to pretend to be invisible, but in being invisible to others. The shaman's wife had cooked the food, then appeared not to notice when her husband filled a piece of bark with three-quarters of the shellfish, and left. She had continued eating her share at the fire, not looking in the direction he had gone, or appearing to notice the sounds of eating a few yards away. After half an hour he returned, ate what few she had left, and then gestured that they should return to the beach. She led the way, so that Jangamuttuk could signal the boys to stay hidden at the edge of the undergrowth. They stayed behind, but spied on the adults who were going to the ghost and the strange man from a faraway country who had passed through the same initiation process and was thus a young adult, though to them he seemed almost as old as Jangamuttuk.

Fada was still unable to recall his last train of thought and conversation, and so fastened on the arrival of the couple to begin a subject dear to his heart. He declaimed in his sweet voice of reasonableness that he knew swayed his sable friends. 'You see,' he smiled at Wadawaka, 'they are under my protection and care. What with the recent influenza epidemic and the general feeling of lassitude, we are just getting back on our feet and any disruption would only cause a relapse.'

It took Wadawaka time not only to chew over the statement, but to digest it. It threatened to give him diarrhoea. He considered that the way the commandant went about things was criminal and answerable in the famous court of British justice, which had sentenced him without much thought, to wherever this place was. It was more than forty days and nights over the ocean; and more than forty days of squalor and brutality. If only he did not have prison hanging over his head, he would burst his bonds and tell the white devil what he thought of his methods; but a drowning man must clutch after a straw, and so he needed to hang on to this empty tube which was threatening to sink him. What else could the victim do but nod his head, not even trusting his voice to articulate agreement?

The commandant accepted this and smiled as he pontificated: 'They must be led gently, gently into the promised land of civilisation. I do not use coercion. Do I, Ludjee?'

Ludjee was ready with her instant: 'You good to us, Fada.'

Wadawaka's eyes flashed, but he kept his peace. He had been with Ludjee and listened to some of her story.

She had suffered in much the same way as African women had, but seemingly bore no bitterness. This was strange to him. His mother hated the white devils. How could this woman meekly turn the other cheek and side with her captor? Perhaps she was being political and biding her time until the 'Yes, Fada' would turn into 'No, commandant, sir!'; but would that ever happen?

The commandant began to bluster about how missionaries were working to bring the light to darkest Africa. It was then that Wadawaka found his voice. 'After three hundred years of plundering and enslaving us,' he exclaimed.

This set the white devil off. 'Not my doing, sir, not my doing. We have fought for you and what is more we won the fight . . . '

And he went on and on, and the African, after thinking that it was somewhat ridiculous to win a fight after setting up the conditions which made a battle necessary in the first place, let his mind drift away. Once he had believed in their fine words along with the others. The white Baptist minister who had converted him was much like this one—given to resounding words. They listened and believed when that white devil had crowed that they were free. Ill-versed in rhetoric, they took it that there was no more slavery and their joy was boundless. The magic word freedom spread like wildfire, but when they found things remained the same, they believed that the planters were denying the law. They abandoned the hated plantations and flocked together, marching towards the chapel of the minister who had declared that slavery was finished. These were his words. What else could they mean, but that they were free at last. 'Praise the Lord,' they shouted in jubilation as they danced along two thousand strong. And what did the white devils call their jubilation? an insurrection! They entered the town. The chapel was in sight beyond a bridge. They came to that

81

bridge and the red-coated soldiers were waiting. A volley
downed scores. They raced forward angered beyond
measure and the white soldiers fled. Only one of the
white devils had been hurt, but by a misdirected ball
and not by anyone of them. Still, it was enough. Worse,
the minister chided them for their joy and bid them to
return to servitude, to plantations which were occupied
by an enemy out for revenge. They shuffled back to find
the heads of their women folk jammed on stakes. Where
was the Christian justice of it, and where was this
freedom? Only in the hangman's noose, and on the
gibbets which lined the roads. At last even the minister
suffered and had to take refuge on an American ship.
He had been guided there by the still faithful slave,
Wadawaka. And what had happened? The poor
misguided rebel became the personal servant of the
minister. Promised his freedom when they reached
London where all slaves were free, the slave was arrested
as a rebel as soon as he stepped ashore, flung into captivity
and after due deliberation, was exiled to the furthest
colony of the far-flung British Empire. That was what
had happened to him. And what had happened, and
was happening to these people he found himself living
among, was worse. They had been hunted down to the
point of extinction, then exiled to a barren island in
the hope that they too would soon be no more.

Fada at last brought his apologetics to an end, and
Wadawaka commented with an obscure Ashanti saying:
'See and blind; hear and deaf', and left it at that.

Jangamuttuk had watched and listened to Fada's
bluster. It meant nothing to him. He knew Fada and
could apply one of Wadawaka's aphorisms to the
situation which must be resolved: if duck won't leave
pond, then pond will leave duck. But this time the duck
left taking Ludjee with him, and Jangamuttuk laughed
at his back, then called the two boys down to the beach.

'These two soon to be made men,' he exclaimed proudly. 'First ones for two, three year now. Not too late to begin again.'

Fada had plunged Wadawaka into despair for he believed that there could be no release, and Wadawaka mocked Jangamuttuk. 'How we do that, Obeah Man, how we do that?' he almost chanted. 'You prisoner on this island; I prisoner in this colony. How, you tell me that.'

Jangamuttuk replied, 'Easy, maybe we just sail away. Make these little ones men and just sail away.'

'How do that? Never put match to canefield, for you like be caught in fire,' Wadawaka retorted with another cryptic African saying.

'Water too soft, need earth to put some strength into 'im,' Jangamuttuk mocked in return. 'Soon time come. Com-mand-ant, he says that he is going to take us away from here. In chapel tonight, he want us to sign that milli-milli, paper of his. Strong paper, yes?'

'Strong enough to send me back to that white prison.'

'You come with us when we go.'

'You wouldn't want me along.'

'Well you just come with me. You belong us mob now. Just a little while and you see. Maybe tonight maybe next day—soon!'

'What you mean, Obeah Man? You makes as much sense as I do when I have to speak to that commandant,' Wadawaka replied, unable to believe that there could be any escape for him, or the people.

'Uncle,' Jangamuttuk mocked, though stressing the kin relationship accepted by Wadawaka when he had been initiated into the community, 'I got this way of talkin' from you in the first place. Anyway, you uncle to these boys under our Law. You me same like that in our Law, since I cut you. Now soon you do same to these two boys, but first we have 'nother little ceremony.'

83

'Obeah Man, don't hold with that. It's not straight way of doing things.'

'What's this Obeah?! If you sick you go to doctor, he make you strong. Come, what do you say, man, we put these picknys to sleep. Camp not far away. Up on that hill. Maybe you left one of those sheeps for me. Need lots of food, today, tomorrow, more the day after.'

Wadawaka, still labouring under the burden of his past nodded, then went to the undergrowth. One of the men had dropped off a carcase there. He hefted it to his shoulder and set off after the old man and the two boys. The light was fading fast and he needed what remained to follow them through the bush and up the treacherous path leading to the Obeah Man's camp.

The two novices seriously regarded Wadawaka out of the corners of their innocent brown eyes. Wadawaka returned their gaze. He thought of the ordeal they were about to go through and made sure that they received as much meat as they could eat. Jangamuttuk allowed him to do this, though he made sure that the prohibition on speech was maintained. In this, he knew that the outer forms were being kept, though he had doubts about the whole initiation process itself. Away from his own country, it was difficult to fit ceremony to action. Ceremonies had to be performed at the places where the ancestors had created them. These were the strong places which generated the energy to infuse the ritual with the sacred. Now in seeking to keep to the old ways in this fresh land, he was creating new ways. This was all he could do, for although the entrance to the skyland was blocked, new ceremonies filtered through into his dreams, and these his people accepted. The old and the new mingled and continued though this was the only strong site on the island and the dance areas he had laid out were on barren ground devoid of power. Still, whatever doubts he had, the process of initiating boys had to be maintained to keep the ceremony strong. After, they might reach other countries with stronger sites where the initiation could be empowered. He stared at the novices for a long moment. He could not deny them the ceremony. With a gesture he ordered them to stretch out beside the fire and rest. He thought of the ordeal they were about to go through, then switched his attention to the water man.

Wadawaka stirred uneasily under the gaze of the Obeah Man. He twisted in his sleep finding no comfort in his dreams. Not only was he an exile, but he had no country, no land of his own. All that he had was the ocean moving under him, moving and groaning and carrying on all the time. No rest for a body anywhere. Even those who drowned had no rest. They floated deep beneath the surface, and vagrant eddies moved their hair or beards. They seemed to be alive, their clouded eyes staring out at him, demanding, never satisfied. What did they want? Wadawaka came out of his doze and still the Obeah Man was glaring at him. Half awake, he saw him take two thick pieces of wood and drop their ends in the fire. The flames licked at the dry wood and began eating into his eyes. His mind was all aflame as a voice, which was no voice, imparted a story to him:

'In the beginning there was no fire for our ancestors. They huddled cold and miserable under a biting rain. Everywhere damp moist, wet, cold! Nowhere warmth, the needed warmth that would move the blood through their veins. Then in the bleak expanse of fog a single spot began to glow. Slowly, slowly, they dragged their bodies along their sight to it. Each by each, they took turns sitting on the spot. They felt the needed warmth. They took it into their bodies, one by one. Slowly, their bodies began to become supple. Each by each, they sat over the spot, and it began to increase, in warmth, in brightness. Warmth became heat and our ancestors tended the site. As the area glowed with heat and energy, the rain eased and the fog retreated. The original spot was far too hot for them to bear. They moved a distance away and left one of their number to observe the place where the warmth had been born. One time, the guardian of the warmth saw a rising of what he took for vapour, then a reddish—how to describe what was never seen till that time—fire came into being and as it flamed the fog dissipated. Now each ancestor took part of that original fire for himself. And the passing of fire from generation to generation continued to this day, and the original site of fire still remains under the care of its guardian.

'Now when our ancestors were increasing the warmth, some places on the outskirts of the world remained beyond the reach of the heat, though eventually the inhabitants of these cold places stole fire. It was not the fault of our ancestors that the warmth stopped spreading, for the site of warmth had become too hot for them to increase, but the denizens inhabiting the cold areas blamed our ancestors for not doing so. They accused them of keeping the heat and warmth to themselves, and over time they began to hate the humans. The terrible cold continued on in the ghost land, and the denizens there finally found a way, through a great and evil magic, to capture the souls of the humans who had died. Part of their plan was to close off the way to the skyland and they succeeded. To this day it remains closed. No shaman has had the skill to force the passage and so a split has occurred between our ancestors and ourselves; with disastrous consequences such as our present predicament. Worse than this, however, is that the souls of the dead humans linger on in the ghost land.

'Leached souls, white with pain, huddle together seeking the warmth of rebirth, huddle together for the warmth of the healing fires of the skyland. But there is no release, no hope and no warmth. Only the coldness turning them into frozen brittle vapour. I, Jangamuttuk, have flown to the land of the ghosts. I have sat with those who have gone before. I have talked with them, and listened as they told me of their pain. I promised to help them, but the shining road leading to the heavens is blocked and I do not know what magic chants and ceremonies can open it. Then I sought the lower road, the warm richness of the tunnel leading to rebirth. It also is blocked and the souls have no release that way. The necessary conditions have been wrenched apart. I have not been able to bring them together to permit souls to take bodies. So bad has it become, that we are dying out, and soon all that will be left of us will be a collection of leached souls in the ghost land. Worse, still worse, the ghosts by their magic have wrenched the very planes of existence apart. Where once there was a unity and a wholeness, a going from one to another freely and easily, there has become a resistance and repulsion. The strong men and women, the shamans, the *mapans* need to come together to restore the health of the world; but they are disappearing in the broadening chaos. It is the end of an age and the slow dawning of another.'

'Come,' Jangamuttuk called loudly to the barely conscious African, then laughed as the man's large body shivered and sank into a wakeful dreaming state which made for receptivity. Jangamuttuk pulled the two blazing brands out of the fire and thrust one into the man' hand, then with a muttered chant, he guided him through the narrow cleft behind the camp site. It seemed to widen to allow them egress, then tightened behind them.

A comforting warmth surrounded Wadawaka. It felt so maternal that he almost regressed to that state of being a baby unhappily clasped to his mother's breast—before they tore him away from her. How he cried and cried.

The sugarcane juice was his tears. Sweet tears that made a strong bitter drink which turned strong men into unconscious infants sheltering in the womb. Unable to feel, unable to think, unable to walk, only to totter, to crawl; unable to sing, unable to talk, unable to stutter, shout, cry—bubbling helplessness of the womb being, which he was. Safe at home in the womb. Feeling the warm walls constricting; feeling all the hurt receding; feeling, feeling, sadness sweeping, bitter the taste, bitter the womb, pressing walls pressing, pushing, pushing into a world of of of . . . his father's arms about him. Arms he had never known. Holding him firmly and seeking to protect him from all hurt; but hurting still. Hurting, hurt, the pain inside at the loss of his father. No slaves had fathers, or mothers, or sisters or brothers. Draught animals kept for their work. No, not human beings at all, and the devils can go to wherever they live and the souls must be given warmth, warmth, love and forgiveness to all, allowed to flow through to all the planes. The ways must be opened. Bitterness and hatred block the way through to the empowerment of a doctor. Bitterness is a pain to be excised; hatred is a pain to be excised; slavery is a pain to be excised; the son replaces the father and waits for fatherhood. The ancestors seek to come and participate. The way down is blocked. The present generation is cut off and must make its own decisions. Judge that the time is ripe as the candidate is ripe and naked as the hard steel point of the assegai stabbing down and down as death lies in wait and smiles and snarls at the pale forms eager for the kill, while behind them other souls shudder at the kill. There are the gates to open, the passages to be burst through. Pressure strains and the cold souls shudder. The seals hold and there is no more waiting for the kill.

Obeah Man drops from the stone ceiling and moves

him along a sea lane filled with the decayed shipping of a thousand nations, all seaweed covered and breathing out sighs as the tropic warmth floods away the cold, and pale bodies bake a living brown in this far colony, far in the future when his body has long since been lacerated and ripped apart. Now he is the particles of dust being tossed to and fro by warm water on a sunny beach as . . .

An *abeng* sounded a long blast which stretched far over the ocean, carpeting it with flowers and his mother's seldom laughter. Drums clicked into the chirps of prison craziness and then rolled away the walls with the snigger of despair. Sudden despair stretched his body out as crucified as the ocean, dead fish tugging at his massacred hands and feet. His crown of thorns slipped and his forehead healed as a line of song came from his lips. He repeated it, then another and another. Triumphantly, he sang out his chant, adding it to his rhythm and to the rhythms of his people now remembered. Strong the connection. Crystal clear the outstretched cord, rolled up and rolling, and all was hidden never, forbidden and loved by the shamans' vow to keep all a secret. It belonged to him and was secreted in his very body cavities. His organs were removed. His beating heart, his spleen, his kidneys, his liver, his bowels, even his lungs. His body was a bloody hollow and even that disappeared. Now it was a butchered carcase, empty and cleared of fragility. How could he see it when he was it? Now new organs of crystal began to replace what had been taken away. Built up inside, his body shone with the whitest of translucent light, and then the dark skin was gently folded over as a new song verse began.

Lines began forming over his body. Wavy lines marking out the pattern of his, his totemic animal— the one which he had never been given in Africa. The lines thickened into irregular blotches laid down in a regular pattern. He tried to trace out the stylised pelt, then a warm tongue lapped at his cheek and he eyed the savage face of his spotted companion, Leopard. Again the rough tongue ran over his face, and he felt the energy of his totem flowing into him. Now the night sky beckoned, the deep, dark forests beyond, and he sprang up and onto the back of Leopard, who sprang immediately into the air, feeling the unrestraining hand of his rider on his neck, feeling the unrestraining hand of his rider running along the powerful muscles of his shoulders and he sprang through the air, sailing high and fast and free.

Flying high and free. The peak of the hill below him, the cleft a vagina cut into the living rock. The hidden cave glowed and then from the cleft, as if ejected, came leaping a fearsome dragon shape; a giant goanna with a tiny figure lying on its back. It was as if man and creature were one. Leopard glanced behind and snarled in a teeth-baring display of ferocity which undazzled Goanna. He came sailing on and slowed to take up a position beside Leopard, who relaxed his guard and actually purred. Wadawaka looked across and smiled at Jangamuttuk who took up his clapsticks and beat out a steadying rhythm. Wadawaka found his *abeng* stuck through the hair belt which, apart from the pubic shell, was all that he wore. He had discarded his clothing, or had had it removed during the initiation ceremony. He raised his instrument to his lips and let it give forth a long blast, then added three whoops of his own joy. As the last of the sounds tapered off, the boom of a conch sprang a challenge at him and his companion. The sound seemed to have a form and substance of its own and rose and fell about him as if seeking an entrance into his self. Both Goanna and Leopard became uneasy. Goanna hissed and Leopard snarled. Jangamuttuk clasped his sticks and beat out a rapid rhythm, and then

90

they were racing through the air at a tremendous rate, pulled towards the boom of the conch. Jangamuttuk clicked out his rhythm and Wadawaka lifted his *abeng* to his lips and let it follow along with the rhythm. The instrument had a voice of its own and bent notes about the steady booming of the conch. Tendrils of fog began rising about them. The booming suddenly stopped and they turned and fled. Wadawaka darted a glance behind him. A strange bird with huge flapping wings was in rapid pursuit of them. It was steadily drawing nearer and in a moment would overtake them. Wadawaka began to panic. Such a monster looked too formidable to fight. He moved Leopard closer to Jangamuttuk for protection. The shaman flashed his face towards his companion and changed the rhythm of his clapsticks. Wadawaka, recovering his courage, raised his *abeng* and blew a challenge, then they turned and flew straight at the monstrous flying creature.

VI

Fada had not had the best of days. In fact it had been a fragmented period filled with alarming gaps and pieces of his own sentences commencing and drifting off into chaos. If he had not been a scientific person of the nineteenth century out to use the weapon of calm rational thought against all superstition, he would have been inclined to blame his befuddlement on the machinations of the devil; but machinations, or machines were the work of man, and as a humanist, he strongly believed that man had no reason to truck with the devil. To be sure he was aware that there were dark areas within his own mind; but what science did not explain by theory and experiment, he looked to religion to explain, and to suffuse his being with light. Naturally, he strove to accept his Christianity as an example of rational thought, which science would eventually prove beyond all doubt. He knew that it might accommodate the notion of the devil, but what was the devil compared to the all-seeing, all-knowing God, the Father above who filled his days and nights with light and love. These were both aspects of a scientific theory which was even then in the process of being formulated according to strict rules which left no room for devils of any description. The Science of Christianity was an all-encompassing wave spreading rationality ever outwards. What were the dark beliefs of savages, but areas where the wave had not yet reached, or penetrated. He was on the pinnacle of that wave, sweeping away all those hellish practices which were only the childish notions of souls without divine grace and rational thought.

Fada breathed deeply and easily, aware of how he possessed the dialectic of truth. As light and darkness were opposed, so were the victorious forces of civilisation ranged against those of savagery; a savagery which was everywhere in decline. He breathed deeply again, then fell into alarm as he failed to find the train of thought which sustained his complacency. How and why these lapses were occurring, he had no idea. To whom could he turn with the nearest doctor five hundred miles away? It was one more reason to leave the mission. He needed medical advice, and perhaps treatment; but the colony's doctor was a quack. If only a more enlightened physician were in port. He made a mental note to seek out such a physician, then as his thoughts were on matters medical, he let his mind drift onto the nature of his wife's illness, or rather illnesses, for she complained of a bewildering number of symptoms which at first had alarmed him, before merely presenting a puzzle for his scientific mind to unravel.

Women, he knew, were subject to mysterious visitations of illness. In fact, a ruder age had put them down to the machinations of the devil, or even possession; but that was before psychology had shed its light on the somewhat overheated and fragile mind of the female, so prone to vagaries and irrational notions. Similar to children, they needed strict guidance and control, for if left to their own devices, they were apt to forget their stern duties of kitchen and nursery and wander off into flights of feverish imagination. A certain 'wandering' was an inclination of the female mind. If not controlled, reason was lost as it drifted off into fantasy which might end in insanity, or worse, vice of the most depraved kind. In the case of Mada, he had sought to strengthen her rationality. He had denied his household such instruments of downfall as the romantic novel, and had populated his bookcase with edifying works. He even

93

had left his bookcase unlocked so that she had access to it whenever she desired. What more could he do? It was not his fault that she seldom availed herself of his library, for besides the more stimulating and useful literature, which might not appeal to her female mind, he had the complete works of Sir Walter Scott, which were or should be, romance enough for any mind. After all, he was a knight writing about other knights in a royal pageant firmly resting on the stern morality and code of behaviour which had made the English gentleman what he was. But did Mada even pick up one of the volumes? No sir. Again he sighed, then fell to contemplating the nobility of Sir Walter's style. 'What a wordsmith, what a wordsmith,' he exclaimed. He would have liked to base his own style upon it; but the scientific nature of his own work forbade it, though, though, perhaps (indeed it was more than a thought), perhaps his masterpiece might benefit from a warmth of prose style which would appeal not only to the arid mind of the scientist, but to the rhetoric of the evangelist.

This was such a discovery that it pulled Fada out of his evening meditation which he conducted in the sanctuary of his office, while he was supposed to be working on the next report, including the costing of the mission. Usually, he put off doing the accounts for as long as was possible, or until the last minute when Mada roused herself to put them into some kind of order.

What pained him about the whole subject of accounting was the fact that there was no income from the mission. This fact he couldn't avoid. Two columns and one absolutely blank. No income, and this had to be remedied. How? He must encourage the natives to manufacture implements and tools (suitably improved by himself) to be sold as amusing artefacts for profit. Already there was a ready market amongst the earnest Christians in England who, now that slavery had been abolished, were ready to turn their full attention on the poor, but noble savage. Now, he must add that to his report and embellish it. It was just what was needed to show the flourishing state of the mission. True there had been setbacks, but didn't this prove that things were improving, and that his natives were at last ready to bring others of their kind into such institutions where they would learn the habits of industry and, and . . . He searched for the word to cap it off, but his mind was a blank, or rather filled with thoughts of·hunger. It was near the time of the evening gathering when his family would sit down to a frugal repast. As the head of the household, he must be on time.

A new moon sickled the sky and Fada stood admiring the night. Above him sparkled the Southern Cross, and from it, a shooting star. There it went and it struck the summit of the mount which towered over his mission. Yes, it certainly had, and that would bear looking into on the morrow. If it could be found, it would be a discovery of some note. He must send the natives to scour the slopes for it. They had little enough to do, for the fields which he had planted with corn were now a mess of bracken, owing to neglect occasioned by the recent contagion. The task of clearing the bracken and replanting the crop must be undertaken soon; but it could be left for another day. Now if the meteorite could be recovered, he would dispatch the singular object to the learned gentlemen of the Royal Geographical Society. He could even adorn his report with an appropriate native fable of fire falling from the sky. It was too good an opportunity to be missed, and he could compose the report on the vessel taking him to the town. Highly content with his lot, he entered the bungalow.

A neat and washed Sonny sat in his proper place to the right of the head of the table. It was as things should be. He nodded at his son, then frowned as he took his seat. Mada's place was vacant. He sighed a deep sigh as his wife slowly entered from the kitchen carrying a large platter on which a row of very lean mutton chops and some withered potatoes lay congealing in a lumpy gravy.

'Don't blame me; don't blame me,' she snapped as she let the platter fall with a thud which shook the table. 'It's that slattern Ludjee. She hasn't put in an appearance. It's just too much for a body.' And she collapsed smouldering into her chair without a glance at her husband.

Fada's sense of contentment wilted in the atmosphere of her rancour. He opened his mouth to remonstrate, then clenched it shut.

The evening meal was a period of social disharmony and tough meat. Fada blunted his knife on a chop, then finally giving up any pretence of good manners, picked up the wretched bone and began gnawing it. Mada flashed a glance of contempt at him, then gave up on the tough meat and sawed the dried up tubers into dainty enough pieces for her mouth to chew on. She dreaded what they would do to her stomach. She envisaged them there defying the copious spraying of the digestive acids, until her intestines spasmed in painful rejection. It was too much. She gave up on the vegetables and cast a venomous look at the oaf of a husband who continued his swinish assault on the bone. Only the fruit of their loins, Sonny, blessed with youth, a cast-iron stomach and a palate which had never known anything but rough colonial fare, enjoyed the food. Lasciviously he eyed the last chop congealed in the dripping and flour gravy. He glanced at his father. Would he or wouldn't he take that last chop?

Fada flung his bone down with contempt, scraped back his chair and after commanding Sonny and his wife to follow him as soon as the table was cleared away, stomped through the door apparently on his way to the chapel. Outside he spoke curtly to Ludjee and walked rapidly to his office, unlocked the door, closed it behind him, then unlocked a locker in which he kept the mission supply of rum. He poured himself a half mug and gulped the fiery liquor down in one long vicious swallow. After this he measured a small amount into the bottom of the mug, tasted it appreciatively, then slumped into his chair and thought thoughts as bitter and as hot as the liquor. How he wished that he had never had Mada forced on him. A wife should be the left arm and hand of her husband and here she was thwarting him at every turn.

'Have that last chop dear,' Mada said to her son, feeling that she had to be motherly to her strapping lad. 'You have to keep up your strength to bear the likes of him,' she couldn't resist adding, then relented: 'Now I'll just be off and make you a nice cup of tea.'

She smiled at her son as he greedily scooped up the last chop. She knew that after that he would scrape the platter clean, and so there was time enough for her to have a sip of her medicine. It was more than a body could bear. Fancy to have to put up with that beast day after day, week after week, month after weary month. No wonder she was so thin and fretful, and her agony was more than enough to make one long for death. She took a mouthful, then another. This was all the comfort she had, and all thought of making her son a nice cup of tea left her as she fell to sprawl on what she fancily called her bier. Well, it might be; but there was none of that nice finality which she had seen in one of Sir Walter's books. She wished for such a departure from this vale of sorrows and slid easily into a dream where she felt that she could be free and away from the stings of that bully pretending to be the Christian gentleman. 'How soon his sweet words had turned to vinegar,' she murmured as she left the wretched mission on what she hoped would be waves of euphoria. To help herself along, she began singing in a wavering little girl's voice:

'In innocence I once did love,
In all the joy that peace could give,
But sin my youthful heart betrayed,
And my fate is worse than a convict maid.'

Ludjee had accompanied Fada to his office but had been quickly dismissed. She had watched with dark eyes which showed nothing of her thoughts as his portly body pushed through the office door. 'At last,' she sighed, and turned to retrace her steps along the track to the beach. She went to the water's edge and sat down on the soft dry sand. The tide flowed towards her. Little waves ran up and stopped just before reaching her knees. A larger wave flopped and spread beneath her body. She leapt up with a girlish shriek and flung off the heavy shrouds of her ghost clothing. Freed from the constricting cloth, she felt her body take in the wind blowing from the sea and smelling of sea things. She stood still. The ocean rose and fell, rose and fell in time with her breathing, in time to the pulsing of her blood. She felt herself flowing out to become one with, and yet apart from the great waters. She wanted to dive beneath the thick swollen surface and feel again the strong back of her companion arch up beneath her. She gave a low moan which flung her face up towards the sky. There the cradle of the moon man hung glowing and empty. He had gone to be with his brothers, or they had come and taken him. Still the boomerang shape hung there, a sign that he would return round and glowing from the rich fatty meat of the feast. She felt her lips move. She was hungry, but hungry also for the other thing. Both could be satisfied under the waters.

She sat and rested, breathless with expectations. Then

she began breathing rhythmically, letting the rise and fall of her breasts become synchronised with the rising and falling of the ocean. The waters foamed towards her, tumbled over her lap, until she got to her feet and began wading out. A wave foamed about her knees, another reached her hips. The third swept her feet from under her. She struck out, swimming strongly away from the island prison. Her mouth gaped open like that of a fish deprived of its element. She gulped down as much of the cool night air as her lungs could contain, then she dived down and down, and up and up as her Dreaming companion took her body. Now she was above the waters speeding south. Ludjee stroked the leading edge of Manta Ray as she dipped around in a great circle before heading them back towards the island. Smilingly, she relaxed, and stretched out fully on the broad back. She surrendered to the feel of the air on her bare skin, and felt herself become part of the sparkling darkness.

Manta Ray trembled under her and she awoke to find that they were above the central ridge of the island. She thought a request; her Dreaming companion hovered over the summit, then dipped down to circle the great boulder under which her husband had set up camp. No thought rose from him, but her heightened senses picked up the agitated breathing of the two novices. Now, she knew, was the time for them to be made men, for they were on the verge of rebelling against the silence and the enforced inactivity. But where was her husband? She raised her conch and blew a deep moaning cry at the moon cradle. As if in answer, came the far rattle of clapsticks, followed by the blast from what Wadawaka called an *abeng*. Ludjee stroked her companion and she sped off along the sound of the blast. There, illumined by the moon and starlight, she saw Jangamuttuk and Wadawaka on a Dreaming companion she had never, never seen. In her mind there was no image except that of a dingo, reforming into the shape of Mada's cat which they had caught and eaten when the supply ship was long overdue and their supplies had run out. The Dreaming companion was similar to it; but magnified a thousand times and it looked as mean as that cat had been when they clubbed it to death. It gave a snarl as Manta Ray raced near, then the snarl fled as Jangamuttuk tapped out a rhythm of welcome. Wadawaka added his horn to the rhythm, and she trembled out an answer. Manta Ray flew on and the others formed up on either side. They sped on.

The thin plane of the familiar buckled and flowed. The cool night air reeked with the odour of rotting flesh, and then they were through. Ahead, the peaks of the mighty ghost dwelling rose, threatening them with its icy radiations of despair. Ludjee shuddered. Her mind filled with images of the skeletons of her butchered community erected and on display as if, as if . . . savagely, she raised her conch and answered the bitterness with a warm woman's cry. Hot as a crystal needle long held in the hand, it sped out to release its warmth on the ice of the vast hulk.

Wadawaka stared down into the vast cavern of a ship's hold in which crowds of black men and women lay in befouled rows. From a far corner came the pitiful cry of a newly born baby. In anguish, his hands twisted at the neck of his totemic companion. Suffering as much as Wadawaka, Leopard turned angry sad yellow eyes towards him. Inexperienced and at the mercy of the forces of the ghost world, Wadawaka slipped into the shell of the small boy sitting on his mammy's knees as he listened to her bitter words. The scene shifted, and down below was the white devils' fortress in the depths of which his mother lay imprisoned. Her anguished voice called for release; called for him to save her. He sought to answer back in a strong man's voice which issued forth as a thin wail of a poor lonely waif. Then he and his companion dived to the attack in spite of Jangamuttuk's clapsticks beating out a rhythm of caution. The other two experienced shamans touched their mounts. They glided down after him.

Leopard extended his paws as he came in for a landing on the battlements of the grim castle. He found himself sprawling on a mirror smooth surface of ice. Desperately, he clawed for a foothold, then snarled as his razor sharp claws failed to scratch the smooth hard ice. It began to burn him through his pelt with an ice cold vacuum which sucked up his strength. From within the stronghold, a low hum began. It caused the battlements to tremble as it rose in pitch and volume until it was a shrill whine which pierced his skull through and through. He lay there completely immobilised, while his rider writhed in agony at the sounds. Finally, there was a release. The whine reached a crescendo which flung him off the battlement. Bled of energy, he felt himself hurtling through the air completely out of control. He flashed past Goanna and Manta Ray. The force clutched at them, and hurled them away from the structure. Worse, as they were swept up, they began whirling around and around and in and in towards the vortex of the cyclone. There hung a giant boulder. They were in danger of being splattered against it as the whine reached a shriek which tore the air past the boulder, then suddenly the noise stopped and with it the wind. Above them, the cradle of the moon swung in the security of infancy. Free of panic, riders and mounts swooped down towards the white peak, or fort, or castle, or? . . . Now each rider clutched a crystal which gathered in the rays of the warm moon and refracted them in streams of rainbow light.

Again, the hum rose to a whine, and again the wind tore at them. A thick cloud formed between them and the moon. Bereft of power, the crystals faded and they were weaponless. Then again the whine dropped to a hum stilling the air. They pulled out of their dive and hung in the sky as a huge form rose from the ramparts, or the ledges of the peak. It hovered below them. A huge ungainly gleaming red body boldly painted with yellow stripes slowly revolved beneath transparent wings. It pulsated with a bluish light which was painful to gaze upon. Multi-faceted eyes glowed with a red fiery light which spread out to search each direction. The light caught them in its glare. The thing began to rise towards them. They saw the deadly sting dripping with luminous venom with which it was armed. Desperately, they raised their crystals, but the white fog hanging above them not only cut off their power supply, but was beginning to descend. It too looked threatening and not a place to hide in. They sought to retreat, but had left it too late. The light from the monster's eyes shifted from red to blue and they found themselves paralysed. They could move neither tail nor fang, tooth nor tongue, hand nor paw. The blue light lifted them up and they sprawled flat and helpless against the sticky bottom of the cloud.

All seemed lost. The monster neared, and then a second ungainly shape left the structure and streaked through the air towards the hornet. It was the huge white dreaming bird which Ludjee and Manta Ray had seen on their last flight. Then, it had seemed wounded and harmless. Now as she watched, feathers streamed from its body until it became all taut white skin gleaming and cold. At the leading edge of the wings cruel talons clutched and unclutched spasmodically, and the long featherless and hairless neck extended out and out to two blue eyes and a long horned beak serrated with teeth. On reaching the monster, she immediately attacked. Instantly the insect reacted and stopped its wings. It fell hundreds of metres, then a high pitched whine began as its wings began to vibrate. Up it surged at the strange bird; but it was impeded by an instinctual bending of its abdomen as it stabbed again and again with its sting. The strange bird was much more manoeuvrable and controlled, easily evading the compulsive stabbing as it darted in to slash away with its talons. The clumsy monster hummed angrily and the hum began building towards a whine, but its attacker swooped through its defences and fastened upon its back. Clinging fast with its claws, it used its deadly wing talons to rip at the multi-faceted eyes. The blue light flickered into red; the building whine faltered, and the monster whirled towards the Earth. The strange bird released its hold. The monster recovered and built the humming into a whine and then into a shriek. With its transparent wings ripped, it wobbled towards the peak, or fortress, or castle. The bird-thing folded its wings and dropped in pursuit.

The white cloud dissipated and the companions were free. Jangamuttuk tapped out a rhythm of energy. The conch cried and the *abeng* wailed. But the sounds were thin and weak. They were cries of shock rather than shouts of defiance. Jangamuttuk and his two fellow shamans sought to summon up the energy lying in the pits of their stomachs. Crystals glowed softly, then dimmed. Their companions feebly fluttered as they tried to fly; but all that they could manage was a controlled descent into an atmosphere reeking with foulness towards a land covered with blood. In ever narrowing circles they glided down to land on ground which failed to support them. Goanna and Leopard sought for a footing, but found none. They began sinking down and down. Ludjee realised the peril they were in. Manta Ray alone was able to move through the fluid. She requested her to move next to Goanna's head on which Jangamuttuk perched. He slid off onto the back of Manta Ray. She then swam next to Leopard and received Wadawaka onto

103

her broad back. Safe, they severed the mental connection binding them to their Dreaming companions who had almost disappeared from sight. Only their heads remained above the surface. Now, these too disappeared from sight. There was a slurping sound and the congealing blood rushed in to fill the empty places. Manta Ray radiated a sense of security over them as she skimmed slowly over the blood, which now they saw was a wide moat surrounding, what to each appeared to be, the white steep cliffs of a mountain peak, or the grim ice blocks of the lofty walls of a castle, or a fortress rising sheer into the sky without foot or handhold. And from this edifice came the same sorrowful wail of loneliness and despair which Wadawaka had previously identified as the voice of his mammy. Now he realised that he had been mistaken, or had been led astray, though the voice was female and perhaps emanated from one who was in the grip of the same devils as those who had ruined his childhood.

Ludjee glanced at him and gestured caution. She raised her crystal and he did likewise. Jangamuttuk began a careful tap-tapping on his clapsticks. Now they were at the base of the mighty white wall. It was impenetrable. Jangamuttuk tap-tapped out his rhythm, and the cradle of the moon appeared floating in all serenity. The rays gathered into the crystals, which flashed. Rainbow light streamed out and through the walls. Manta Ray bent a wing as he carefully moved his body against the hole. They slid off, but as they entered, the light of their crystals faded. They hesitated; but the walls of the tunnel were covered in a mould which softly glowed. The green luminescence was enough and they moved off. Ludjee led the way. At intervals she stopped to blow a delicate breathing through her conch, while Jangamuttuk tapped out a protective rhythm on his sticks. The *abeng* refused to function in the subterranean tunnels. It was choked with mud and Wadawaka had no way of cleaning it.

As they continued, their bodies became coated with the mould from the floor, ceiling and walls. Now they too glowed with the same soft green light as they moved deeper down into the edifice, or into the living heart of the mountain.

Beneath the huge boulder which sheltered Jangamuttuk's camp, the two novices jerked into wakefulness as from above them came a terrific humming. The fire was a heap of glowing coals. They hastily added leaves, then as these caught, some dry sticks and lastly a log. The leaves crackled into flame, the sticks twisted and caught and the fire flared around the log. The rock shelter became filled by eerie writhing shadows in which, they just knew, lurked the terrible old woman who ate young boys. They huddled together expecting the worst. The frightful buzzing grew into a high-pitched whine which rose into a shriek which shook the whole peak. They clapped their hands over their ears to prevent the sound from entering. It set their teeth on edge; but they could not keep it out. Worse, came another screeching sound which, they were sure, was the overhead boulder shifting on its foundations. The fear of being squashed as flat as any of the bugs they had amused themselves with was added to their supernatural fright. They knew they were about to be paid back for their cruelty. The shrieking and screeching went on and on. Finally, the braver of the boys untangled one arm and hand and groped around for the spear their teacher had been working on. He found it and got up to confront, with a badly trembling shaft, the scariest of the shadows.

Then there came a clicking of something on the rocky ground just beyond the reach of the flames. The boy flung the shaft through the entrance at the sound. It struck something and fell to the ground. Quickly, he flung more leaves on the fire, and wished he hadn't. Indistinct figures could be made out just beyond the reach of the illumination. Now their teeth began chattering. The scratching clicked above the shrieking filling their heads. The braver lad, now a panic-stricken boy, grabbed the log from the fire and flung it at the figures. It was battered back at them and landed in the fire, scattering it across the floor of the shelter. The flames flickered and began dying out. It was what the figures had been waiting for. They rushed in and at the lads. So scared were they that they did not even struggle. To add to their woes, they began gagging as a pungent odour filled the shelter. Their frightened eyes stared blankly up at the indistinct figures; in terror the two novices fainted dead away as a giant insect with gleaming multi-faceted eyes lurched towards them.

Mada dreamt that she was in a very expensive and exclusive shop in Bond Street. When living in London, Mada, if she had dared venture inside such a shop, would have been shown the door without any fuss, but now in this dream she was a beautiful lady with the right to try on splendid gown after splendid gown. Not finding quite what she wanted, she reached for a small hat which took her fancy. It fitted tightly over her golden hair. She went to a mirror and screamed. The hat had turned into a mass of glittering beetles. Her hands leapt to her head, then away. She couldn't bear to touch them; but they were touching her. She shrieked again and again as hundreds of tiny claws dug into her scalp and tens of tiny mouths chewed at her skin. She shrieked again and again. No one came to her aid. Then the gown she had left on began to harden and fuse with her skin. She writhed and ripped at the fabric. Her nails broke on the hard carapace. The weight dragged her to the floor and she scuttled off to hide in the darkest corner as a mocking voice intoned:

'Ye London maids attend to me,
While I relate my misery,
Thro' London streets I oft have stray'd,
And now I have been awfully repaid.'

And the carapace melted away and she was a naked soft pink thing, pelting along a darkened street. Above a sickle moon gleamed, then vanished as fog rolled in, and she was elsewhere. She became a maggot thing which inched along narrow corridors the same diameter as her body. She writhed on, then grew many legs and scuttled on away from the click, click of insect claws on cobble stones. She was on the darkened street. Her shape changed and swiftly she raced up a lamp post. She exuded a strand of web from her abdomen and swung upon it. A wind spun her across the narrow street to another lamp post. She fastened the strand, and began a web. Her work was perfect. She smiled as she settled into the centre. Soon the prey would blunder into it and she would feed. The thought made her drool. White liquid dripped from her chelicera, fell onto the thickest strands of her web and dissolved it. She began falling and falling. The long strand of silk arched behind her and thickened to become her body. And all the time the click-clicking followed her, coming nearer and nearer. Terrified she reeled her body in and as she fled, shifted from insect shape to insect shape. Still the click, click came after her. Suddenly, there was the soft crooning of, of—her latest form grew gossamer wings before expanding out and becoming a ship from the deck of which a man heaved a fish up from the depths of the sea. He slowly dragged out the agony of the iron hook which lacerated her mouth; set it down and took up a knife. With a swift upward stroke he disembowelled her. Her hot entrails steamed beside her empty body. Rough fingers scraped along her backbone finding more and more of the filth and flinging it down beside her. Disgusted, her mind fled up the thick fingers which dug deeply into her gutted body. And all the time there was the click click clicking, all the time that soft airy moan as if from, as if—and she was flying high above the mission, spreading skin wings which gleamed silver under the sickle moon.

She trailed a silvery cord as she flew. It stretched back to that gutted body now lying abandoned on the heaving deck of the ship which was also her body. She flew on into a great storm of rage that grew talons along her wings; then she heard the crying of a child, then another and another. Her miscarriages re-entered her body, then emerged as spirit children which sped from her out and out into the sky. She rushed after them and into a zone of desolation. Her beak opened and she gave forth a cry of longing. A groping hand knocked over the flask of laudanum. It shattered on the floor and the liquid dripped through into the mug of rum which Fada sipped as he dreamt of a new and more amenable wife, or helpmate. She fled from him trailing the string of her miscarriages behind. Each one the result of a passionless encounter. The click-clicking followed hard on her, near her, above her . . . The airy sound persisted and penetrated her body. She felt herself being reeled back; being reeled back into the mire of a past life which laid crystal shards upon the faded carpet of her dreams and nightmares. She fought back wanting to die. Mandibles closed over her wing. She struggled free of a horny mouth. An insect of red and gold abdomen bent and straightened. The sting flashed at her, venom dripping. Desperately, she whirled and flung herself onto the back of her worst fear. The talons on the tips of her wings began raking away at the tough chiton. Savagely, she dug into the joints in the armour. Ecstatically, she saw the spurt of

108

green juices begin to erupt, to cover her with slime, gently glowing. But still she clung to that back while her wing talons dug and dug into its eyes until the monster faltered in flight and began to fall.

She saw that one of its long clawed feet clutched a sack. Now in its death throes, the foot jerked open and the sack fell free. She separated herself from the dying insect, and folding her wings fell after the sack, caught it and soared upwards and towards the forest. And all around her was a shrieking and beneath her was that click-click towards which she glided down and over a patch of clearing in the forest. It was rimmed with evenly spaced fires and the clicks came from it and the shrieking came from the darkened forest, and from a near oval-shaped clearing came a droning which soothed all her hurt. The cord of her miscarriages was severed and dropped into a fire which began blazing in the centre of the clearing as she swooped low over it. She might have landed, but there was a hiss which slashed through the other sounds. It was followed by a snarl which caused her to imagine teeth and claws sharper than her own. A huge goanna and leopard stood on each side of the fire. The leopard lashed its tail and the goanna flicked its tongue. She flapped her wings and began ascending to get above the treetops and away. As she did so, she let fall the sack, and then soared high on huge wings which began to grow soft feathers. And she was back in her bed writhing as the ballad began again, but this time to comfort her:

'Far from my friends and home so dear,
My punishment is most severe,
My woe is great and I'm afraid,
That I shall die worse than a convict maid.'

The tunnel seemed never ending. Worse, as they continued, it began to close behind them. Dismal was the oppressive atmosphere which seemed never to have known hope. A keening of infinite sadness permeated the air and they breathed in despair against their will. Ludjee tried at intervals to press back the gloom by repeating the gentle sighing on her conch and Jangamuttuk tapped out the song from the ghost ritual, then softly chanted the verse:

'They made of me
A ghost down under,
Gave me a dram,
It tasted like cram;
Real as my dream,
Way, way under.'

The walls pressing in on them receded. They found themselves in a cavern filled by a lake of clear water. Jangamuttuk, being unable to swim, hesitated; but Ludjee stepped to the edge of the pool and slid into the water. Almost instantly, she felt the strong back of Manta Ray rising beneath her. Gently she ran her hand over the head of her Dreaming companion. A wing fluttered to acknowledge her touch. She beckoned to her two male companions to slide onto the back of Manta Ray. They did so, lying down and tightly gripping the wing edges as she began swimming slowly through the water. They streamed through the water and at last reached the opposite shore. The water had washed them free of the green mould, but another source of illumination had replaced the luminescence. The pink walls of the cavern radiated a warm humidity which glowed over their bodies lovingly.

As they proceeded, their feet became heavier and heavier. Ludjee raised her conch and blew a plaintive note, which Wadawaka tried to match on his now clean *abeng*, but the instrument felt as heavy as a hogshead of salted pork and dragged his arm down, and down, and down. He felt the warm dark body of his mother pressing him to her. With a trembling sigh, he sank into her embrace. How peaceful, how utterly peaceful everything was. At last he had returned to the source and there was no longer any sense in struggling, or living. He slumped to the ground and curled up into a ball. The smile of a contented infant sweetened his face. His breathing slowed and he began sinking into a coma.

Ludjee stared down at him. She felt her own legs beginning to give way under her. Walls, floor and ceiling pulsed rhythmically. She began sliding into a warm sense of well-being in which there was no separation between inner or outer. She was the walls, the ceiling, the floor—pulsing slowly; pulsing rhythmically. A click-clicking threatened her sense of unity. The warm flesh of her body broke asunder from the warm flesh of the floor. A feeling of utter loss overwhelmed her, then Goanna darted his tongue at her. She became that warm blue tongue.

Jangamuttuk held on to the rough skin of his Dreaming companion. Strength flowed from him to replace the lassitude. He tugged Ludjee onto the broad back of Goanna then dragged on Wadawaka. Their hands hung uselessly and Goanna had to walk at a slow waddle to prevent them from slipping off. The pink illumination and warmth trailed away as the cavern narrowed into the mouth of a pitch black tunnel. Goanna moved ahead steadily and increased his pace as he felt the hands of the three shamans grip his skin. Ahead there was a snarl as Leopard scouted ahead, his keen senses alert for danger.

Goanna finally reached the waiting Leopard and stopped. Wadawaka slid off his back and went forward. The tunnel terminated in a blank wall of panelled wood. He ran his fingers over the wood at the height of his waist, and touched a knob which turned under his

111

fingers. The door swung open on a room gauzy with a misty white light. Goanna was too large to pass through the doorway. He jerked his head around in search of enemies, but felt none. Jangmauttuk dismissed him. Leopard was also too large to fit through the door; but he shrank his body until he was the size of a small cat. He sprang through the doorway and stopped just inside. The air was musty and a smell of decay tugged at his nose. He gave a tiny growl. Jangamuttuk clicked his sticks and began an improvised verse of the ghost chant.

'Made me made me mad
Sad ghost place face
Ghost ghost ghost
Sad face place lace.'

He changed from the ritual verse into a protective chant as he glimpsed the figure writhing on the bed. It was white and gauzy too. Tendrils of hair floated about a ravaged face and skeleton body. Ill-health lay there almost ready to be interred, but life slept on, for the breast fluttered. It was a female ghost, one that had caught some contagion and became imprisoned in this room. Suddenly the female jerked into a sitting position. Her blue eyes sprang open and she uttered a cry of despair filled with a hunger not to be denied. Now her fang-like teeth began gnawing at her pallid lips until they were lacerated; but no blood came. Now her hand moved like some insect towards a bottle which Jangamuttuk on his last visit had mistaken as the elixir of all health. It was, he realised, a deadly drug responsible for the prison in which the poor female lay. As her hand touched the flask, he struck it with one of his clapsticks. The flask hit the floor with a crash and shattered. He watched the evil liquid soaking into the faded floor covering which held some interesting designs. Jangamuttuk had no time to examine them closely, for the ghost turned a gaze as cold as the ghost land outside and the mouth began drooling a misty liquid. Skeleton hands clutched at the gauzy fabric that covered the bed. She writhed in an attempt to rise. It was then that Leopard leaped upon the bed purring and snuggled up to the awful apparition. The hands ceased their spasmodic clutching. One was pushed out to weakly stroke the warm fur. Leopard purred on, and the female ghost relaxed.

Wadawaka brushed his way through the cobwebs of thin material which floated, filling the whole room. He reached the far wall and came upon more substantial material, thick white curtains which hung from ceiling to floor and which might hide a window. He tugged at the material and it came away to reveal a small window tightly closed against all outside influences. It had not been opened for a long time and the hinges were rusted over. Finally, he managed to create a crack wide enough for his fingers to slip through. He lent back and jerked. A flow of cool night air entered. Then the rays of the crescent moon reached through to silver the chamber. Ludjee stared at the pathetic figure: 'She very very sick that one. She needs crystal medicine.'

Jangamuttuk bent to examine the patient. She was breathing so slightly that the material which covered her breasts barely stirred. He touched her skin. It was icy cold. He picked up a wrist. The pulse moved without energy. He saw how her incisors worried the bloodless lips in a hunger of the heart rather than of the stomach. There was no feeling of well-being, just agony in the wasted form which hungered for her own homeland far away. He looked at Wadawaka, then nodded at Ludjee. They gestured and the crystals appeared in their hands. It was Ludjee's suggested treatment. The rays of the moon gathered and the rainbow light streamed out to bathe the female. She entered into convulsions as the light pierced through the pores of her skin. Her skeleton was

113

outlined for an instant, organs flickered into relief, then became invisible as the rainbow light moved over her skin. Her breath began rising and falling in the deep rhythm of sleep and her skin lost it pallor and became flushed with health. Leopard gave a contented purr and sprang off the bed. He stalked to the window, sprang onto the sill and then off into space. The trio went and looked out. Leopard hovered there. Wadawaka climbed through and onto his back. He flew off and his place was taken by Manta Ray. Ludjee climbed onto the back of her beloved companion and she flew away. Now Goanna waited for Jangamuttuk to mount him. The shaman looked down at the broad back and the faded markings. He really must touch up those patterns. Then he jumped on and clicked his sticks in a jaunty rhythm. From the forest came answering clicks followed by the deep droning of a didgeridoo. Ludjee answered with her conch and Wadawaka blew a blast of victory on his *abeng* and their mounts turned and made for the forest.

VII

'Strong drink has always been the unhappy lot of our class,' a more than slightly inebriated Fada thought before repressing the statement. In truth, he was forced to ease his problems with the application of that strong drink which he had no qualms in condemning when used by others; but then he had always seen it as a medicine which, on occasion, was a necessary prescription to relieve his overtaxed body and mind; a body and mind absolutely devoted to a work which was more and more, not less and less, clouded by suspicion and innuendo in the chief town of the colony. It really was time to be off, and leave the future to judge him and his works favourably. He sighed and finished his drink. He looked at his watch and saw that it was past the hour for the important church service and the signing of the petition pleading that the Government should evacuate the station; but not in a piecemeal fashion. It might be time to conclude his noble experiment on the island; but withdrawal had to be dignified. The shepherd must lead his mob of sheep towards new fields of endeavour. He sighed again. His thoughts filled with a fresco of himself surrounded by his adoring sheep, chief among whom was the nubile Ludjee. He sighed again, and got to his feet. The room whirled around him and the floor reached for his face. He recovered his senses and balance. Dignity had to be maintained at all costs.

After carefully locking the empty rum bottle inside the cabinet, securing his office door, and checking to see that the store's door next to his office was locked, he turned to survey his kingdom. The castle of his domain

115

rested in darkness. He hoped that Mada and Sonny were patiently waiting for him at the chapel door. The church was his pride and joy, an enduring monument to his living faith. There it stood dominating the compound in solemn majesty. And in darkness! The whole compound lay in darkness. Only the livid stars and the unfeeling new moon shed some light on his mission. He had sacrificed everything for these ungrateful savages and how had they repaid him? With an ignorance that was almost overwhelming. And an absolute indifference to his philanthropy and mission. At best, he had given many of them Christian burial; at best, he had baptised the sickly infants; at best, he had forced them to repeal their savage laws enforcing a beastly coupling and enter into the bonds of holy matrimony, and so, and so, his work was not in vain. No, for there had been victories. The women now covered their nakedness with demure skirts and the men wore trousers. Satisfied, Fada strode to his chapel, where he startled his lounging son, who was sleepily digesting the toughness of the evening's meal.

The two novices regained their senses and dropped into a shallow pit. They clung together, finding security in each other and the soft earthen walls pressing against them. They were afraid to examine their surroundings, and shudders racked their bodies when they thought of what had happened and might still be in the process of happening to them. After what seemed ages, light began to pass through their tightly clenched eyelids. It calmed the boys and gave them enough strength to flutter open their eyes. A circle of blazing torches illuminated their pit and above them concerned faces gazed down at them. Like two young animals, they clung to each other and stared up, their wide open eyes flickering in the dancing flames. Then mouths opened to begin a

116

soothing keening. Strong motherly hands reached down and pulled them apart and out of the pit. Limply, the novices were passed from arms to arms. They were hugged and petted until they were completely smeared with the women's body paint of red and white.

At first still in shock, they accepted the women's ministrations, then they struggled to escape the smothering bodies. All the time, the soothing keening continued seeking to calm them into aquiescence. Soon, they could no longer resist. After months of isolation with the often irascible Jangamuttuk and his constant admonitions to remain hidden, their sudden discovery and reclaiming by the women, by a motherhood which they had thought lost with their childhood, undermined whatever self-possession they had managed to maintain. Unable to cope with what had been a kidnapping by monsters beyond their wildest nightmares and the replacement of that terror by an overwhelming love beyond their softest dreams, they succumbed to insanity. They fell into infancy. Their hapless cries rose above the female keening, which continued on until the two novices fell asleep safely clasped in mothers' arms.

Fada flung the chapel door open and ordered his son to light the lamps hanging in brackets around the walls. Sonny, with a lighted taper, went from lamp to lamp. The increasing illumination only served to show the empty pews—pews which he had had to bargain for in long pages of correspondence—and now, it could make a body cry, they were as empty as his wife's head. If he wasn't who he was; if he had not been endowed with a mission, he would close up this empty building and return to his office. No, that would never do; but what to do? He ordered Sonny to take the large brass handbell which rested on a table just within the door—he had spared neither himself nor his cash to make this a fitting house for the Lord—and ring it long and hard. As the peals began, he ascended the pulpit and slumped over the railing before pulling himself together and surveying his church.

'Lord, let them return in penitence,' he whispered. As if in answer, from the direction of the forest came the keening of female voices overladen with the powerful cries of infants demanding to be loved and cuddled. Their demands were met, for the cries died away as the sounds of the bell died away. In the church, silence remained to tug at his mind with desolation. And from the forest continued to flow the keening of the women. Perhaps there had been a birth. Perhaps that was it. They would never forsake him. He was their, their saviour. Soon, they would return to joyfully sing the hymn he had taught them. Perhaps it was the time to teach them another. How sad that the recent contagion which had swept his mission had put a stop to everything. A detailed program of instruction and education must be placed in operation; but, but, sadly, it would have to wait until he returned from town. He and the Lord knew that his son was utterly incompetent to further his Christian mission; and as for his wife . . . Well, she was better left out of any plan. And why wasn't she here? No wonder the natives were lax in their religious duties. It was all too much. He glared at Sonny who had seated himself at the back of the chapel in the very last pew. Well, it would have to do. A congregation of one was congregation enough, for even if only two were gathered in the name of the Lord . . .

He picked up his hymnal, tapped it on the edge of the pulpit to get his son's attention, then thundered: 'We shall begin this evening service with a hymn, no. 358'. Lustily, he began singing the only hymn that he had taught the natives. He hoped that they would hear it and come to the building. His son joined in enthusiastically. It seemed that the whole chapel quaked as they yelled:

'From Greenland's icy mountains,
From India's coral strand,
Where Afric's sunny fountains
Roll down their golden sand,
From many an ancient river,
From many a palmy plain,
They call us to deliver
Their land from error's chain.'

The urgent and sustained pealing of the bell upset the women. Their keening faltered, then rose shrilly. The mothers of the boys clasped their sleeping forms fearfully in their arms. The rest of the females began a dance about the two mothers. The only accompaniment to their keening was the shuffling of their feet. A rustling began in the undergrowth which surrounded the boro ground. The women faced away from the mothers and began a faster step. The keening rose. The low hanging boughs of the trees were being violently agitated, as on the wind came Fada's shouted words:

'In vain with lavish kindness
The gifts of God are strown,
The heathen in his blindness
Bows down to wood and stone.'

The wind gusted and the words fled from the forest, back whence they had come. The hymn was drowned and replaced by a whining, building up to a roar which completely overcame the women's voices. They stopped and backed into a tight circle about the two mothers. Branches snapped and boughs bent. The weak moon slid behind a cloud and the encircling fires which the women had lit with their torches flickered feebly. Then came the massed cracking of clapsticks beating out a marching rhythm of the ghosts. The wind turned and struck at the fires. The flames fluttered wildly and stamping through the chaos came grotesque dancers, their bodies dripping with white pipeclay. They danced towards the women and away, then came rushing at them. The roaring which had descended to a whine rose again into a monstrous voice calling for bloody sacrifice. The white-covered figures violently danced at the women, and the female circle broke. Before it could reform, the males were at the two novices. They grabbed them. The women shrieked and tried to prevent the men from taking the boys. There began a ritual tug of war. The men tried to drag the boys away from the women, while the women tried to keep them within the protective circle. The female keening began, but this time filled with a shrill anger which tore at the dull roaring. The men hesitated, and the women began stamping in a dance of their own. They circled the two mothers and the infants. They appeared to have won. Then the leader of the male dancers produced a pistol, aimed it at the women and pulled the trigger. The explosion ripped away the women's dance and song. They froze. The males snatched up the boys and bore them across the boro ground to where an entrance to a narrow passageway through the forest was marked by two fires.

Fada opened his mouth to begin the third stanza which he knew and loved so well. Then, at that precise moment came the sound of a shot. A pistol shot! It had been near too. What did it mean? No one except himself had firearms on the island. He had expressly forbidden it. His mission was one of peace and love. He did not need the power of soldiery and the musket to bring the natives to heel. No, just as they had become reconciled through persuasion, they were to be civilised through kindness and example. So there were no other firearms on the island, but the brace he kept locked in his chest. Now could the natives have got at them? No, he had instilled in them a mortal fear of guns, and then no one except Ludjee was allowed in the bedroom where he kept the chest. So it was not one of the natives who had a pistol, and that meant . . . He refused to accept the dreadful picture which flashed in his mind. His pistols must have been stolen, and possibly by that African. His mind refused to accept this easy solution. The man never, ever entered his home, and Mada, yes, Mada spent most of her time in the bedroom.

'Sonny,' he commanded with less assurance than usual. 'Have you been at that large chest? The one I keep locked in my bedroom.'

His son merely looked bewildered. Now the awful truth had to be faced in all its stark horror. It was the end of him. It meant the loss of all that he had striven for. He could never live it down. His enemies were waiting for such an opportunity. If only it had been a native uprising. Stand firm and expose his breast, if need be in a holy martyrdom; but this, but this . . . The terror of his situation drove him in panic from the chapel. His son got up from his seat, made to go after him, then thought better of it as his stomach gave a long low growl of discomfort. He settled back. It was the last chop that had done it.

The women stopped their shrieking as from the passageway two figures daubed all over with charcoal leaped to confront the white devils. As Jangamuttuk and Wadawaka began a dance of defiance, the women turned and left the clearing. Their part in the ritual was over and they were not allowed to see the remaining portion. They began a song of joy as they walked back to the meeting. Ludjee led the singing:

'In innocence I once did love
In all the joy that peace could give,
But sin my youthful heart betrayed,
And now I am a Convict Maid.'

With red ochre-encircled eyes blazing, the two shamans threatened the devils with their bare hands. The white devils gave a loud laugh, and began a dance of their own, miming what they were about to do to the two men. Behind the main body the boys were being carried across the backs of two of them. The dancers stamped back around them triumphantly, then the leader waved his pistol and with a wild yell charged towards the two shamans. Jangamuttuk and Wadawaka quickly produced their crystals. They held them over their heads as the moon floated free from the cloud. The glistening yellow ochre reflected rays down, to be concentrated in the crystals, and released in a flood of rainbow illumination.

'Mada, Mada,' a breathless Fada managed to cry, as he entered the door of the bungalow. One hand was clutched at his pounding heart, and he had to wait all of ten seconds to recover from his dash. He hurried as fast as his tired legs could be driven to the bedroom. He hesitated a long second outside the door dreading what he would find. He flung open the door. 'Mada, Mada,' he blustered, as he found his wife calmly dressing herself. 'I thought, I thought,' he stuttered, suddenly overcome with an emotion he identified as relief.

His helpmate met his eyes calmly, and her nose slightly, ever so slightly wrinkled. Just a few hours ago, she would have cut him with a 'been at the rum again, eh!'; but somehow it didn't matter so much. When he had entered the room, he had appeared so concerned, that it might have set her to laughing. She wondered what had set him off. He was such a silly sometimes. After all the years together and she still found him as immature as the day they had met. Why Sonny appears steadier, she thought as she smiled at her husband. Well, what else could be done, but stick it out? After all, they had been through a lot together, and no one was perfect in this world, and so she smiled at her red-faced husband and said apropos of nothing, or of what was upsetting him: 'I'm sorry if I disturbed you. I was just getting ready for church and accidently knocked my bottle of medicine there. You wouldn't have believed it, but it sounded like a shot,' and she gave a girlish giggle which managed to get through the pompous ass to the Cockney lad still lurking beneath.

The effects of their long isolation and their recourse to rum and laudanum occasionally caused them to shed their affectations and to see each other as they once did, when they were young lovers in London years ago. These happy interludes were infrequent but brought an element of pleasant unpredictability to their otherwise combative relationship.

As they both giggled and cuddled, from the forest came the sound of clapsticks and the droning of a didgeridoo. 'I know you hate this hell of an island. I feel that it is time for us to prepare to leave this, this work of mine which is near completion. For you it was a time of suffering, but for me it was a chance, a chance well taken. Mada, there are other fields to plough.'

'And streets to walk through and cities to see. This island—so deserted and forlorn. Somehow it grips my heart only now that I know I shall soon be leaving it. Oh, I'll miss that, that . . . '.

'Those rude airs which somehow . . . '

From the forest came Jangamuttuk mimicking Fada's voice in song:

'They made of me
A ghost down under,
Made for me
A place to plunder,
A place to plunder
Way down under.'

Husband and wife looked at each other, then began giggling wildly.

The two novices regained their sanity to find themselves being carried along the passageway across the shoulders of Jangamuttuk and Wadawaka. Jangamuttuk felt the boy he was carrying begin to stir and said over his shoulder: 'Maybe you thought becoming a man was kid's business, eh? Bit more than that, eh?'

The boy did not reply and from behind Jangamuttuk, Wadawaka answered: 'We got both of 'em now. They belong to us now.'

Jangamuttuk laughed and said: 'An' men don't cry. So don't go snivellin' and wettin' my shoulder. And they don't go runnin' to mummy either.'

Wadawaka shifted his burden, and joked: 'Naw, you go running to the girls instead.'

'Though you better watch out,' Jangamuttuk replied, then added: 'Anyways you won't worry 'bout that for while. Soon you'll be a little bit less than you are now.'

'It's that little bit you're holding on to now.'

'Anyway, you gotta become less to gain more.'

'You two are going to be marked men.'

The passageway opened into a small clearing. The devils began dancing around them. Wadawaka and Jangamuttuk led the dancers around the clearing, then cut across to the platform of boughs which had been constructed in the centre of the clearing. They gently placed the two boys down and covered them with two blankets. Jangamuttuk tucking in the blanket around the novices' heads commented: 'This'll be the last time you'll be out of sight. Just one little thing to be lost. This is it.'

Wadawaka laughed as he replied: 'Can't be calling 'em boys after this. They gotta have new names. I'll call this one George 'cause he looks a bit like that old crazy king.'

Jangamuttuk lifted the blanket off the boy's head, then carefully examined his face, before answering: 'And this one'll be Augustus. New names, ghost names, signify something you know. Best we get the business done. Throw some green boughs on that fire. We'll give 'em a good smokin' first.'

For the first time in years Mada was happy and even felt comfortable in Fada's company. Soon, she would be back in London. She just knew she would. The very thought made her giggle. No more island, no more colony, no more way down under. She looked at her husband and their eyes met. His reserve crumbled and he returned her giggle with a laugh. He too felt freed from a burden which had bowed him down long enough. The stagnation of island life was not for him. He had left his mark on the island and that was more than enough. Praise the Lord, ahead was the church he had built. Soon, it would stand a lonely beacon. Perhaps a solitary fisherman would land and enter to worship. Perhaps it would prove a haven for shipwrecked sailors. Whatever use it might be put to, it would always remain a monument to his work on the island. Before he left, he would have to place an engraved plaque on the building. If history was to be history, it had to be signed and thus secured for all time. If he left the church unsigned, anyone might claim the building of it, and that would not do; would not do at all.

Mada waited until her husband assumed his customary position some yards ahead, then followed. As long as he was leading her in the right direction (which was off the island) she would follow. They were halfway across to the chapel, when Mada heard women's voices singing lustily. She recognised the melody, and called to her husband: 'Why how nice, they are singing my song.'

Fada was overjoyed. They were flocking to evening service, albeit rather late. 'Praise the Lord,' he turned and smiled at Mada, then frowned: 'But, Mada, this song is quite unsuitable for this occasion. There are processional hymns which might elevate the spirits of the natives as they troop to church.'

Mada couldn't help retorting, 'Some have other ways of lifting their spirits', but then was instantly contrite.

Knowing that the ceremony of adulthood was proceeding correctly, the women had left the boro ground and had washed the paint off their bodies before donning their mission clothing. The splashing with cold water had raised their spirits instead of diminishing them. Ludjee mimicked Mada's voice as she led the singing. They entered the mission compound and were surprised to see the church all aglow with light. It was midnight and they couldn't understand what Fada was up to. Perhaps he had been waiting all this time for them. Ludjee was surprised to find Mada and Fada standing together in the centre of the compound. They seemed as happy as if they had just made love. It was strange, strange indeed. Their singing trailed off. They bunched in an embarrassed clump.

Fada forgave them their intransigence, overjoyed to find that his faithful flock had not deserted him yet again. Instantly, he took charge of the situation: 'It's well that you are in fine singing voice. We'll begin with . . . '

But the final words were drowned out by the boom of a cannon. At last, the supply vessel had arrived. Fada turned to Mada and said: 'Praise the Lord.'

To which his wife replied: 'Praise the Lord indeed.'

Fada turned back to his flock and intoned: 'Now, third verse of our favourite hymn, no. 358.' With Fada followed by Mada at the head of the procession, they all entered the church joyously singing:

'Can we, whose souls are lighted
With wisdom from on high,
Can we to men benighted
The lamp of life deny?
Salvation! Oh salvation!'

VIII

And so the road led to the beach and poor Island was beginning to feel that once again he was fated to be uninhabited for some thousands of seasons. When was the last time a sizeable population had wandered over his skin? Ten or twenty thousand seasons ago. He couldn't be more exact, for what was exactitude to an immortal? The seasons succeeded each other in a slow rolling which contrasted with the quick dash of the sun. But now, that slow rolling had been disrupted over the last decade. Where his skin had been tickled by the claws of animals; where it had felt the slow dragging scrape of a seal pulling itself from the water, now these sensations had disappeared. They had been replaced by humans, but even these sickened and died as had the larger and smaller animals. Now his body felt naked, though the forest still remained. Now, the humans were preparing to leave and the last experiment in communal living was drawing to a close in all the disarray he knew to expect from humans. Of course, with these humans there had been a few bright moments, the humorous and even, on rare occasions, the corny; but all in all they were a sorry lot, best taken, if one had to take them, in couples, or singles, then . . . but why theorise, or even think? The wreckage of their lives might be examined at leisure, perhaps when they had become nicely petrified and as solid and reliable as rock.

Mada, perched on top of the pile of luggage loaded onto the mission cart, remembered their horse, Ned, and how he had been killed and eaten some months before. This occurrence was still the subject of government correspondence. She felt that she should be in a state of the wildest exaltation in gaining her greatest wish, in satisfying her greatest craving, her everything of leaving this awful island far behind, so far behind that it would not even be a memory to unsettle her; but, but, but, somehow she felt an uneasiness as if she was about to sink into a state of depression. This was absurd and she determined to be cheery. This, after all, was the natural state to be in. She had gained what she believed her heart desired: the renewed attention (and love) of her husband; the evacuation of the mission and retreat to the main settlement of the colony, which was, (she at least sincerely hoped) the first leg of a voyage which would leave them high and dry in London. There they could live on her husband's pension and the proceeds of his speculation in land which was about to net him a tidy profit.

Island had arranged a grand procession of farewell, and it reminded Mada of the Queen's coronation. How she had longed to be in London at that time when the pride of the Empire was on display. As Island knew, just about everyone loved a procession. Some eagerly entered into the spirit of the occasion, though others refused to take part. Fada, as usual, was trading so heavily on the goodwill of the natives that he was on the verge of bankruptcy. Only the natives had just cause for celebration, especially the shaman Jangamuttuk who it may now be revealed had orchestrated things so that Fada would need to retreat to the capital. How he had done this remained somewhat of a mystery, but Jangamuttuk needed the absence of Fada and the ascendancy of his son to fulfil a certain operation he had in mind.

Fada had no inkling of what awaited his son's regime, as he strutted alongside the sweating men pulling the cart. Of course, he frowned at such exploitation of native labour. He frowned at most things, good, bad, or merely indifferent; but there were always exceptions and today the exception was his departure on a mission of diplomacy to the Governor; and, of course, the recent illness of Mada necessitated her riding on the cart, though no male in his right mind would allow even a healthy woman to walk unaided over the rough ground.

Beside him proudly walked his faithful companion, Jangamuttuk, though his old legs found it difficult to keep up with even a leisurely pace. Poor old chap; he had steeled himself to accompany his old mate on what might be their last journey on this Earth. Fada sighed deeply and fondly glanced to where Ludjee, his other faithful companion, walked beside her husband. Ah, he remembered when she was but a young lass entering the full bloom of her womanhood. His glance filled with envious lust. How could she, how could she? . . . Quickly he directed his emotion into safer channels.

Rubbing his hands gleefully, though somewhat dubiously, he smiled around at his procession. It was as he had always imagined it—the shepherd at the head of his newly saved flock. Feverishly, he began storing the aspects of the image in his head. It needed more than a quick sketch. It should, and must be, the subject of a painting. He sighed with a deep contentment. 'It is at times like this,' he said, 'that I know that my work has not entirely been in vain.'

Mada listened. God, the cheek of the man, she thought, and in spite of her recent conversion could not help retorting: 'It is at a time such as this, that I call on Sir Walter Scott in thankfulness for my rescue.'

Perhaps, as befitting the occasion, Mada should have reined in her retort, for the alert Ludjee immediately digested the words and spat back: 'We waitin' for you come back, missus.'

Fada, sensing that a misunderstanding might occur, hastily broke in to stop Mada from corrupting the simple faith of his charges: 'Soon, soon Ludjee, we shall return bearing good tidings and gifts for all.'

'Oh my God,' Mada said, resting her case for a while. She found it extremely difficult to completely accept Fada at face value. In truth, he was a travesty which he himself had fashioned out of a Cockney boy whom she had known and might still prefer if she thought about it. But she was unable to keep silent. 'Over my dead body, you will!'

Jangamuttuk had been sidelined for too long a time. The problem with playing the 'poor old fella' is that too often one is taken at face value. Well, Jangamuttuk hadn't got tired of playing that role, in fact he was an old fella, but he wasn't senile. Anyway, the shaman got into the act. He clutched Fada's arm and said pathetically: 'You takin' that strong paper, commandment.'

With a jovial sigh, Fada corrected him. 'Com-mand-ment, no, com-mand-ant, Jangamuttuk. Please repeat it after me. Com-mand-ant.

'Com-mand-ment, eh. You no "ant", Fada, you commandment.'

Fada sighed deeply, and said a quick prayer to the Lord begging that his senses would remain in good repair while he inhabited this mortal frame. 'Never you mind, old comrade,' he said kindly, with the obligatory hand going to the old comrade's shoulder. 'Never you mind. I have that strong paper and I know the Governor shall honour it. I will take you all to a far, far better place.'

Jangamuttuk looked suitably gladdened as he clutched Fada's hand and warmed his heart by saying: 'Now I know that one hymn, and Our Fada prayer, and both from you, commandant.'

'They are enough, Jangamuttuk. They are enough,' Fada intoned, feeling that perhaps it was time to compose his caravan into a pious congregation.

'But Fada, you leavin' us,' Ludjee wailed out.

'Ludjee compose yourself,' said the delighted Fada safely ensconced in his parson persona. 'Never you mind I shall be back to take you,' he slipped in. 'Never you mind, Ludjee. My son, I leave in charge. He will see that you all get your rations. Obey him as you would me. Strive and better yourselves and this island on which you have been placed. Make it fruitful . . .'

Jangamuttuk reacted to the last words. 'Make 'im what fruitful? Land all forest and empty 'cepting for leeches. No kangaroo, no wallaby, no possum on this place—all gone.'

Ludjee backed him up. 'No shellfish on the rocks, Fada. All gone. This island not good for us. It wants us gone too. I can feel 'im. He say that. Go and . . .'

'Be fruitful in and on the right land,' Jangamuttuk shot out.

When his sable friends ventured into unfamiliar territory, or even began to question Fada and his wisdom, he responded with guilt, which made it even more difficult to pin him down. If only he could face these, his sable friends, with an honest heart, if only . . . To escape this line of thought, his eyes darted around and settled on his son striding along on the other side of the cart. 'My son will take you hunting on the other islands. There must be game on at least one or two of them. Yes, that's what he will do.'

Sonny grinned good-naturedly. It was hard to tell if he was agreeing with his father or not. Well, for him, it didn't matter, for Fada, as the natives called him, was on the way out, and he was to be the boss. It would be him who decided things now, though the schooner and hunting parties were good ideas. If he could locate an island with enough game, it would pay to make a run to the second settlement of the colony. Kangaroo skins brought a good price and also it'd give him a chance to get off the island. Good thing he had that African. He could sail anywhere with an accomplished seaman like him.

'He'll keep you in fresh meat too. But you must look after the sheep on the other island. If you take care of them, then, maybe you hunt 'em sometimes just like you did kangaroo. But kill only what you need for food, otherwise soon no sheep.'

Jangamuttuk was highly doubtful of the future of the mission under the son, or anyone else for that matter. In fact he had no plans for the continuance of the mission at all and said: 'Yes, commandant.'

Ludjee jumped in to capture the last word with, 'Fada, knew best for us' which had an air of finality about it. She was ending her connection with him. It was just about over.

The now less than joyous procession reached the beach and the cart bogged down in the soft sand. Fada steadied the pile of luggage and Mada slid down. She stood at his side as he supervised the stowing of part of it on the ship's boat. As the first load pulled away, Fada ascended the back of the cart. He cleared his throat noisily to get the attention of his flock. Some of them were staring across at the ship in fascination at the small capering form of a monkey. As they watched, it sought to run up the ship's rigging. It climbed rapidly, then shuddered as it reached the end of the line tied to its neck. Frantically, it tried to climb, but each time it was jerked back. Others were staring hungrily at the stores piled on the beach. They were under the guard of two sailors who, kindly souls as they were, tossed a plug of tobacco towards the nearest man. The tobacco fell to the sand and lay there. The sailor looked away embarrassed at the way his friendly gesture had been received. Fada, who was unable to get the attention of anyone, at last yelled angrily. All eyes focused on him. He yelled again and all, except

133

the two sailors, grouped around the cart. Satisfied, Fada cleared his throat, extended his arms, held the pose for a long moment, then gestured to wipe an imaginary tear from his eye. This done, he sternly regarded his congregation, with one hand raised as if for a blessing. Humbly, he began: 'My sable friends, it is with tears in my eyes that I leave you . . . '

'We too, Fada, we too,' broke in Ludjee getting into the spirit of the occasion.

Fada frowned, then continued: 'Our times together on the island have not been only of unalloyed happiness. Yea, there have been trying times too. There has been a time of sickness when death walked amongst us smiting whom he must. Even my good wife and myself have not been spared the bite of pestilence and we suffered along with you . . . '

'You good to us, Fada,' broke in Ludjee tearfully.

'Maybe too good for us,' Jangamuttuk added.

Fada glanced from one to the other. His concentration had gone and with it the rest of his farewell address. Worst of all a memory lapse occurred and he hadn't the foggiest idea what he had been going on about. His mouth opened, his jaw hung, then closed. How to end his address? His mind was a blank and into the blankness came the voice of one of the sailors.

'My third voyage on this run. First time, there must've been over a hundred of the poor blighters. On the second, we found fifty starving wretches. Now on the third there's maybe twenty or twenty-five left. What does he do, eat 'em?'

To which came the reply of the second sailor: 'Cor, he can't half talk, can he? If he don't hurry up, we'll miss the tide.'

And the first sailor replied: 'This place fair gives me the creeps. Wouldn't want to spend a night ashore here.'

Mada finally added her penny's worth: 'Finish up,

or we'll never get away. Save the fine sentiments for that testimonial dinner they were talking of giving you last time you were in town.'

Fada, unable to continue, took the proffered way out and completed what he saw as an historical occasion with: 'So my sable friends, I leave my son a hostage in your hands and declare that in sixty or seventy days I shall return to take you away from this dreadful place.'

Ludjee loved a spectacle and didn't want it to end. To prolong the sweet agony, she darted in with: 'Fada, what shall we do without you?'

Jangamuttuk, heartily sick of watching the ghost prolong his departure, yawned and spat on the sand. He threatened: 'Ludjee!'

Fada had the last word: 'My son, he will take as good care of you as I have done. Have faith all of you.'

Jangamuttuk yawned and muttered: 'And you too, Fada.'

Fada, overcome with emotion, went from native to native, taking their hand in both of his. Real tears came to his eyes. The occasion was somewhat spoilt when the boat returned from its second trip and the sailors noisily stowed the last of his luggage aboard. Mada got into the boat and settled at the stern. Fada left the last clinging hands, Ludjee's of course, and got into the bow where he assumed a posture akin to the painting he had seen of Christ walking on the Sea of Galilee. Sailors cursed as they struggled to get the overladen craft afloat. Sonny dashed into the water, gave his mother a hasty embrace, then placed his shoulder to the bow. The son's strength was enough. With a groan, the bow withdrew from the island and floated free. The sailors scrambled aboard and rowed through the cries of farewell from the shore to the ship. Fada and Mada had successfully evacuated the island.

*   *   *

Sonny made his way to the stores and found that two young boys had replaced the departed sailors. He looked at the stores, then at the boys, then at the stores again. Jangamuttuk was watching him and decided that he needed some guidance. He came up to him and said: 'You in charge, Sonny. You boss, now. These my boys, George and Augustus, I put 'em here to look after the stores. Keep an eye on 'em, for you, eh? It's your job now to look after us.'

Sonny stared at the old man, then looked at the two young men and addressed them: 'Aye, George, you too Augustus, we gotta get this lot back to the store. You get some blokes to lend a hand. If it rains they'll get spoilt.'

The two young men looked at Jangamuttuk for instructions. He smiled at Sonny and answered: 'Sonny, these two a little bit sore. They were up at my camp on the hillside. They coming down to the mission when the track gave way. They got scraped something bad. Can't do any heavy carrying just yet.'

Sonny turned and stared at the old man again. He looked away and then replied to him. 'Your place is in the compound with the rest of your people. I won't have you camping up there anymore. Savvy? Now, if you boys are sore, you find some others to do the lifting and carrying. That cart has to be pulled outa the sand and loaded up. I'll help to get that done. You two, or the old man, take this key and go and get the store door unlocked. Then wait there until we come. You savvy?'

'We savvy,' the three answered solemnly.

He held out the key and Augustus took it, then with George coming after him, he waddled off. Sonny stared after him and shrugged. He gestured to the natives who were still standing around on the beach, waiting for the ship to manoeuvre from the bay, to come to him. They came and he directed some to get the cart free and move it to the stores. While he waited for this to be done, he examined the pile and noticed some sheets of paper stuck between two kegs. He pulled them out. They were the inventory. He flipped through the pages, then stared at the pile of supplies as if trying to divine that list and heap tallied correctly. He looked up and saw that the natives were still trying to extricate the cart. He flung the sheets down onto the top of a barrel and went to help them. The wind whipped up the paper and took the sheets out to sea where the supply vessel under full sail was racing towards the horizon.

Jangamuttuk stood beside the pile of supplies. He watched the paper fly overhead and called out to Sonny: 'Strong paper, eh, boss?'

Sonny, his shoulder to the wheel, looked up in dismay. He grimaced and the men laughed. He frowned. It wasn't that funny, especially when he might have to account for all the stores; but then why worry? His father was responsible and would set things right, or at least fix them so that no one would be able to work out what had or hadn't been done. The important thing was to get the supplies on the cart and the cart to the store. It wouldn't be done, if they stood and watched some old papers blowing out to sea. He turned and Jangamuttuk gestured for him to bring the cart to him.

Jangamuttuk from his position on top of the supplies directed the cart to the side of the store house. Sonny tried to get the men and women pulling to bring it to the door where George and Augustus were standing; but they appeared not to understand him. Eventually he gave up, and leaving the old man to organise things, went into the store to shelve the supplies as they came in. Jangamuttuk gestured George up onto the cart. He pointed out the objects he wished to have handed down to Augustus. Other things were to be handed down to others who stepped forward to receive them. A man stepped forward to accept a bale or keg and instead of carrying whatever it was into the store, went around the back. George stared in puzzlement and the shaman grinned: 'Strong paper, eh? No paper, and no cares, eh? Hey, there's Wadawaka. You missed the big send-off for Fada, man.'

'No worries, been working on the schooner. Some of the ropes rotten. A strong wind'll have the sail down in the first gust. You seen any cord amongst that lot?'

'Come up here and paw over it. Maybe you get lucky and find it. Today holiday, eh? Old Fada's gone forever and we go too, quick smart.'

Wadawaka got up onto the cart and began checking over the stores. He found some coils of rope and other ship's supplies. As he was tossing these down, Sonny came out of the store to find out what the hold up was. He listened to Wadawaka's explanation, then had a go at the stores himself. He was after Fada's private order of victuals. Fada had forgotten it in the confusion of his embarking. Well, dad's loss was his gain, and he would make full use of them. At least the schooner would be seaworthy for a long voyage, what with the amounts of spares and cordage that had been sent. Wadawaka had stacked some barrels and bails with the things; but what they were, he couldn't for the world of it decide. Maybe sails, and tar for caulking. Well, ship things were in the province of the African and he couldn't be bothered about them. He found what he was looking for. A large chest personally addressed to his father, and a small keg which must contain rum. Well, it was just what he needed, and if there was still work to be done, the natives could handle it. They knew what they were about and didn't need his overseeing their every action.

'Hey,' he called to Wadawaka. 'You stow that gear on the schooner.' 'Hey,' he called to Jangamuttuk. 'You get all that gear off the cart and into the store.' 'Hey,' he called to George. 'Get off the cart and lug all that stuff into the store.' 'Hey,' he called to Augustus. 'You look after store. Put things on shelves. When everything is in, you bring me key. You savvy?'

'We savvy, boss,' came the refrain.

'Hey,' he shouted his final order. 'Jangamuttuk, get someone to carry this chest up to the bungalow. I'll take the keg. You're all doing a fine job. Don't forget to lock up when everything's in the store. Bring me the key!'

Sonny was used to making a pig of himself when the opportunity presented itself. Now the opportunity was here and lo and behold he was off his grub. He sat all by himself at the dining table in the deserted bungalow and felt like crying. Only the fact that he was a big boy stopped him from blubbering. He had not thought that he would miss Fada and Mada. He had seen their going only as the chance to assert himself. Well, here he was the boss and he didn't feel like one at all. In fact, all that he wanted to do was sit and yarn; but there was no one to sit and yarn with; and no one to tell him what to do, or fill his days with orders. He was absolutely alone, and the solitude became oppressive.

He brightened up, as from the direction of the chapel came the sound of the natives singing, though it was only about midday. For the world of it, he couldn't understand what they were about. Perhaps he should go and join them. No, he would feel out of place. He must be like his father and remain aloof. When would dad return? How long would he be left in charge of the mission? What would he do if the supplies ran low? What would he do if, if . . . ? What the hell, and he raised his cup and drained it. He had broached the small keg of rum and now was on his third cup. Unused to strong drink, the rum rushed straight to his head, and hence the maudlin state of his thoughts. Now drunkenly,

139

Sonny raised his cup and saluted his father: 'We who are about to imbibe salute you, oh Master of the Grog Supply. Good for the old sciatica; good for a touch of the sniffles; good for three months of solitude. Bugger the natives. I'll be fit for Bedlam by then.' He struggled to his feet, lurched to the front door and yelled: 'Ludjee, Ludjee, you come and get 'em me something to eat, eh!'

Ludjee was dressed in a new dress and trotted up to the front door from the direction of the chapel. 'Yes, Sonny, getting it ready now, boss.'

Sonny staggered back inside. 'Well, it better be ready! Why has the singing stopped? I liked it. It was something to listen to. Where's Wadawaka? I want the schooner ready to sail. We'll get a load of skins and take 'em in and sell 'em. All'll get a share.'

Ludjee had had experience with drunks. Most of the experiences had been awful; but hiding her trepidation, she attempted to humour him. 'I'll get 'em singin' again boss. You just sit there and drink. Wadawaka, he out fixing that boat now. Never you mind. Everything right tomorrow.'

'Well, you get me some grub right now. There was something I had to do. Give out the rations. That was why they were at the chapel. Waiting for their grub. First prayer and singing, then over to the store for the rations. Well, they'll just have to wait. Hear that! You'll just have to wait until I'm good and ready.'

'Don't concern yourself, boss. All that done. Done real well, just like your fada taught us. He good man, he was, he civilised and made us Christians.'

'Well I'm a good man too, and I don't recall giving the order. It's not fair, I have to do it, just like dad . . .'

'Sure, you do, but you relaxin' now. I'll just fix you up some of that nice pressed beef that come in on ship. Stop your tummy rumblin' till dinnertime, then cook you something real good.'

'But, but, why wasn't the key to the store brought to me? Is the store locked? I don't like this at all.'

Ludjee dropped the key down on the table. He looked down at it, then slumped into the chair and reached for his cup of rum. Ludjee told him, 'I was comin' with the key. You savvy?'

'I savvy,' and he took a deep swig of the rum, suddenly very aware that the situation was beyond his control. He hated them. They would never treat his father like this.

'Good. Good, Sonny, now I go get that food for you.'

Sonny tried to retake the position by enforcing a joviality he didn't feel. He tried to force Ludjee to have a drink of rum. 'Before you do that,' he cried, 'you just have a little drink with me. Toast my becoming boss. Old Fada gone and new Fada here.'

Ludjee was becoming tired of the young ghost. Jangamuttuk had told her to go and watch him; but he was as big a strain on her as his father. Wearily, she rejected his drink. 'Maybe after I prepare the food. That stuff gets in your head, makes you stupid. No good for work, then.'

Sonny leered at her and shouted: 'Well, I'll just get stupid some more. Get that grub.'

By late afternoon Sonny was completely drunk and desperately in need of company. He staggered from the bungalow clutching a jug he had filled with rum. He attempted to step off the verandah and down onto the earth. He missed his footing and spun around. Only a flung hand meeting a roof post kept him from sprawling in the dirt.

He gingerly stepped away from the post and lurched towards the chapel. The silence was oppressive and he began calling: 'Ludjee, Ludjee, where you gotten to, eh? Jangamuttuk, Jangamuttuk, rations rations! No show, no gettee, eh!'

He staggered across to the door of the empty chapel and fell in the doorway. By a miracle, he managed to keep his jug upright and free from harm. It was a favourite of his mother's, and she would give him hell if he smashed it. He managed to pull himself up into a sitting position with his back against the door. He took a long swallow of the rum, then began sobbing. There was no mother or father to listen or come to his aid. There was no one. He stopped his blubbering and tried to focus his eyes to see through the trees and onto the beach. He saw a patch of empty sea where the schooner had been at anchor. Wadawaka must have moved it closer inshore. He imagined its sleek lines. It was his escape. When things got too much for him on the island, he could sail off to the nearest settlement for a day, or two, or three. No harm in that, and his dad had done it once. It would give the natives training in seamanship. Maybe he should get up and find Wadawaka now. He'd just do that. Sonny attempted to get to his feet. The effort proved too much and he slumped back against the door of the chapel. How quiet the mission was. Where were the natives? Off in the bush somewhere, no doubt. Pathetically, he muttered: 'Dear Lord, three months of this and I'll be useless for anything. Naw, three months of this and I'll be ready for anything.' With a groan, he fell over on his side and began snoring.

Wadawaka had indeed moved the schooner in with the flowing tide. It was easier to shift the stack of provisions from beach to vessel that way. He watched as the last of the natives got into the ship's boat. He had taught them well. If it had been left to the white devils they would be as helpless on the sea as they were on land. The boat reached the vessel's side and the people scrambled aboard. Jangamuttuk with his fear of things watery, cautiously climbed from boat to ship. Safely aboard and feeling the solid timber of the deck beneath his feet, he shouted at Wadawaka: 'We 'bout ready go and find that new world. This one finished. All finished. We go west into setting sun. End up in our promised land.'

Wadawaka examined the pennant streaming back from the mast towards the land. 'Old man,' he declared, 'we go nowhere until that wind swing round. Tide's near enough on the turn, but that wind, he don't want us to go.'

Jangamuttuk stared at the pennant and laughed: 'Easy enough thing to do. That wind same as cousin to me. I make him turn.'

'You do that, and I'll get a boat crew ready to pull us out of the bay.'

'You get your fellas in the boat and I'll get my fellas together.'

Men tumbled into the boat and rowed it to the bow of the schooner. Wadawaka passed down a cable and saw that it was attached to the stern; then he got some of the remaining men to begin raising the anchor. While they did this, Jangamuttuk tapped out a rhythm on his clapsticks. A man on the didgeridoo filled his cheeks with air and began passing a gentle flow of air down the pipe. The clapsticks began a faster tempo and he began a series of abrupt barks rising out of the soft breathing drone. 'Be gentle,' Jangamuttuk commanded. 'Don't want a storm blowing up. Later we have real ceremony. Say goodbye to our friend. Nice old bloke but he wants to be by himself. There, that got the ear of my cousin. Now he wants to follow us. See!'

The pennant drooped, then lifted to point away from the shore. Wadawaka signalled the boat to begin towing the schooner from the bay. 'Get ready to hoist sail,' he yelled to the men who had been manning the capstan.

Jangamuttuk felt his senses slipping. His clapsticks

changed the rhythm, the didgeridoo followed, and the men began chanting:

'*They made of me*
A ghost down under,
Made for me
A place to plunder,
A place to plunder,
Way down under.
Now we're bound for South Australia.'

The cradle of the moon glistened as it swung over the schooner heading at full sail towards the west. Behind it the central ridge of the island stood out of the water. From the vessel came the tap-tapping of clapsticks and the deep droning of didgeridoos. From behind and above the vessel came answering taps. They met the rhythm from the vessel and changed it. Carried along with the clapsticks came the soft sweet moaning of a conch shell and the blast of a ram's horn. Jangamuttuk smiled and ran his fingers over the weathered skin of Goanna. Again, he had forgotten to bring the paints to touch up the designs so faded in comparison to those on his own body. He glanced across to where Ludjee sped on Manta Ray and tapped out a welcome which she answered with the conch. Unlike his own ancient mount, hers was sleek and glistening dark under the half-moon. A blast from his right marked his rhythm and he saw Wadawaka on his spotted mount. Such a strange animal, but a companion from another dark land. And Wadawaka's body designs were as bright as those of his mount. Suddenly, Jangamuttuk felt old. Perhaps even as old as Island to whom they were returning for a final mission. He stared ahead and with his heightened vision observed a huge white bird swooping low over the mission compound. Its red beak quivered out plaintive cries. Ludjee answered them on her conch. The bird homed in on the sound. She ceased her circling and sped over the sea towards them.

She swooped around them and took up position beside Manta Ray. They came in low over the mountain and down towards the mission. Jangamuttuk saw the reason for her distress. Sonny lay sprawled in the doorway of the chapel; a pathetic bundle of an infant mewling helplessly up at the soft cradle of the moon. The strong feeling of a child in distress swept over them and distracted them from their goal. Wadawaka caressed the neck of Leopard and he left the formation to hurtle down. Briefly, he hovered over the wailing infant, then extended his claws, picked him up and flew along to the bungalow. Wadawaka slid from his back, gathered up Sonny and carried him inside. He tucked him up in his mother's and father's bed and left him sleeping fitfully. It was all that he could do. The giant white bird had landed at the door, and now satisfied that the baby had been taken care of, she flapped her pinions and rejoined the formation. Jangamuttuk tapped out a command. Wadawaka leapt on the back of Leopard. All four now flew to the deserted site of Jangamuttuk's camp. They circled it once, then separated to the four directions of the compass.

Jangamuttuk tapped on his clapsticks and the others answered. Crystals suddenly appeared in their hands. The white bird held one in her mouth. The crystals concentrated the rays of the moon and flashed them down in a powerful white light towards the base of the boulder. Under the onslaught it shifted a little. Beneath it the cleft of Island spread apart. The white light of the crystals faded a little; but a counter flash of ruby red light erupted from a huge crystal which had been hidden deep within the earth and been held captive by the mass of the boulder. Now it gathered the rays into itself and pulsed with energy. The mass of red light hit the heavy mass of the boulder. It began to move, slowly at first, then gathered speed as it rolled down the steep slope at the foot of which lay the mission compound. A deep furrow marked its passage. Trees and undergrowth were crushed beneath its weight. It reached the mission compound, flattened the cemetery and rolled onwards. Fada's monument to history, the chapel, stood directly in its path. The huge boulder pressed it into the earth. All that was left was the square outline of what had once been a church. Island had reclaimed the structure to examine it at his leisure. Now the boulder reached the sea and sped into the water. It slowed a hundred metres offshore and stopped: a monument to the awesome powers locked within the earth.

With a plaintive moan the giant white bird sped down to the mission compound. Ludjee followed. The cry turned to one of joy when she found the bungalow unharmed; but she was not satisfied until Ludjee dismounted and checked to see that the infant still slept. Now both returned to the others, Manta Ray took up her position; but the giant bird glided around them in a huge circle of farewell, then headed south. They watched her with their heightened vision until she reached the supply vessel battling high seas and contrary winds. She hung over the mast for a moment then disappeared. The three riders and their mounts turned their attention to the place where the boulder had once been. The huge crystal now pulsed with a pinkish light which became white. The light was directed upwards towards the Milky Way. As they watched, small sparks of luminescence floated along its length and beyond into the sky. Then the cleft in Island began slowly to close over the glowing crystal. Now the soft light of the moon illuminated only a bare scar in the hill slope. Far off from the sea came the sound of a didgeridoo which was answered from Goanna by the rattle of clapsticks.

146

Leopard gave a snarl as Wadawaka raised his *abeng* and gave a loud blast. Ludjee hesitated, then touched Manta Ray. She sped down and flicked the ridge with a wing as her rider moaned a farewell to Island, who now that the presence of humankind on and under his skin had almost ended, settled back to a peace only marred by the single slumbering boy. The dismal period was over.

END NOTE

Perhaps a few words on the further history of our characters may be in order. Mada unfortunately never returned to London. Upon reaching the chief town of the colony she fell prey to her real sickness. Her simple headstone, which Fada had erected, may still be seen in the cemetery there. Fada survived his wife's demise, the resulting uproar at the destruction of his mission, the escape of his wards and the loss of the schooner. But as he had done in the past, he turned adversity to his advantage.

Such was the magnitude of his blunderings that he was granted a pension, though he was denied possession of the lands on which the mission had stood, even when he offered to buy the island for a halfpenny an acre. He arrived back in England very much the gentleman. He courted and married a young lady, the daughter of an accountant, joined the Ethnological Society and toured Europe. As to his projected volume, this was never finished. Perhaps the energy loss resulting from having a young wife on whom he sired two daughters weakened him. Whatever it was, his published works from the latter part of his life consisted only of a volume of indifferent verse.

Sonny was stranded for six months on the island. His sanity survived, and he managed at last to reach the island on which the flock of sheep pastured. He claimed both island and sheep and the claim was never disputed. He became a quaint and unlovable character notable only for a fondness for rum. As for our band of intrepid voyagers, their further adventures on the way to and in their promised land await to be chronicled, and will be the subject of further volumes.

WILD CAT FALLING
COLIN JOHNSON

Wild Cat Falling is the story of an Aboriginal youth, a 'bodgie' of the early sixties, who grows up on the ragged outskirts of a country town, falls into petty crime, goes to gaol, and comes out to do battle once more with the society that put him there. Its publication in 1965 marked a unique literary event, for this was the first novel by any writer of Aboriginal blood to be published in Australia. As well, it is a remarkable piece of literature in its own right, expressing the dilemmas and conflicts of the young Aborigine in modern Australian society with memorable insight and stylishness.

'The story is...an imperative challenge to the society that breeds his kind.'

Mary Durack, *from the Foreword.*

THE INITIATE
JUSTIN D'ATH

Joint winner of the Jessie Litchfield Award

Stephen Quintus is young, white and middle-class, unsure of his future and dissatisfied with his present. Rafael Roebuck is black, a college student, lonely in Melbourne's white society, and yearning to be back among his people at the Aboriginal Corpus Christi Mission near Alice Springs.

Stephen's life changes when he takes up an invitation to manage the Mission club and learns that if he is to be accepted into the community he must pass a fundamental test: he must become a Man. Rafael, too, must make the transition, but his test is far more complex: he must be initiated, and this initiation has a double edge.

The Initiate is a deeply satisfying, intricate and powerful portrayal of two very different lives and sets of beliefs and what happens when they converge.

PERSONAL BEST 2

Stories and Statements by Australian Writers

EDITED BY GARRY DISHER

Why do writers write? How do they craft their stories? What do they value in their own work?

When the first *Personal Best* volume appeared in 1989, it broke new ground—here were thirty outstanding short stories chosen and introduced by the writers themselves.

The response was immediate and enthusiastic. The *Sunday Herald* called it 'a brilliant collection'. The *Australian Book Review* said the authors' notes were 'full of intimate detail, hard thinking, quirky humour and incisive criticism'.

Personal Best 2 offers the same rewards: brilliant stories and absorbing insights into the writing process.

Stories by: Janette Turner Hospital, Rosemary Creswell, Rod Jones, Geoffrey Dean, Gwen Kelly, Brian Dibble, Jane Hyde, Antigone Kefala, Damien Broderick, Kerryn Goldsworthy, Inez Baranay, Kris Hemensley, Barry Dickins, Marion Campbell, Vasso Kalamaras, Brian Matthews, Peter Cowan, Marion Halligan, Judy Duffy, Ania Walwicz, Laurie Clancy, John Hanrahan, Michèle Nayman, Thomas Shapcott, Nicholas Jose, John Morrison, Marian Eldridge, Amy Witting, Bruce Pascoe and Peter Corris.

THE FAR ROAD
GEORGE JOHNSTON

Imagine the entire population of Melbourne abandoning their homes and taking to the road in flight from the city...

This was how the then war correspondent George Johnston described the Sino–Japanese uprising in 1944. From personal experience came his novel, *The Far Road*, a powerful story of war in China.

Amidst a landscape of corpses, two foreign correspondents, the American Bruce Conover and the Australian David Meredith, set out on an assignment into the interior of drought-stricken China. There they find the population in a state of panic—not from the invading Japanese, but from the local officials.

Through Johnston's self-critical and sensitive protagonist, David Meredith, 'hero' of *My Brother Jack*, *Clean Straw for Nothing* and *A Cartload of Clay*, George Johnston exposes the essential self-interest, not only of the role of the war correspondent, but of journalists in general.

THE BABY-FARMER
MARGARET SCOTT

Have you never heard of a baby-farmer? They trade in children, sir, and grow fat on human flesh.

Terrified that her children will fall victim to the operators of a murderous racket that flourished in Victorian London, a young servant-girl pleads for help in rescuing her baby son.

She sets in train a series of mysterious and shocking events that transform the lives of the dissolute Colonel Fellowes and his family; the sinister Mrs Hartshorne; and a cast of other characters who lurk in the shadows of the richest and most hypocritical city on earth.

The Baby-Farmer, Margaret Scott's first novel, is based on the horrifying facts that emerged at a murder trial in the 1870s. A fast-moving story of crime, lust and greed, it will hold the reader spellbound all the way to its astonishing climax.

MEDIUM FLYERS
PENELOPE NELSON

A top job and national fame were bad enough, but a top job, national fame and a millionaire were an unforgivable combination. Triple whammy. This was what was meant by being lonely at the top. There just weren't enough members of the sisterhood with the same sort of prominence.

Roxane Rowe, at a crisis point in her career, is tempted to sabotage the woman who gave her a start in the travel business. But fate turns the tables, and Roxane finds herself in the hot seat...

Set in the travel industry, an investigation bureau and a number of exotic locations, this fast-paced, ironic novel about women and work asks what a 'medium flyer' has to do to reach the heights of the corporate world.